PRAISE FOR

A Changed Man

"Here is a novel that captures America at its most hilarious and dreadful. Here are characters as richly drawn as any in our fiction to date. And here is a work filled with such keen detail and emotional resonance that every page is a revelation. Come see why Francine Prose is one of a handful of truly indispensable American writers."
—GARY SHTEYNGART, author of *The Russian Debutante's Handbook*

"At once funny, scary, and profound, this novel offers a remarkable understanding of some of the darker recesses of human character. . . . One of Francine Prose's best books."
—CHARLES BAXTER, author of *The Feast of Love* and *Saul and Patsy*

"A compelling read, passionately and compassionately told."
—RICHARD PRICE, author of *Samaritan* and *Clockers*

PRAISE FOR

Blue Angel

"Sheer delight. . . . This is among the most enjoyable books I've read in a long time and, once started . . . I couldn't stop turning the pages until there were none left."
—MICHAEL DIRDA, *Washington Post Book World*

"A blisteringly funny yet compassionate novel. . . . As for the author, she never makes a single wrong move."   —*Newsweek*

"This is a gorgeous novel . . . that not only had me laughing out loud but also writhing with suspense."   —SCOTT SPENCER

PRAISE FOR
Francine Prose

"A world-class satirist who's also a world-class storyteller."

—RUSSELL BANKS

"Prose has an amazing flair for depicting our cultural fallout. Perhaps what's most remarkable is her ability to describe both the miraculous and the decadent in the same bitingly funny tone."

—*Chicago Tribune*

"I know of no other writer who is at once so funny and so unsparing. Francine Prose is one of the most astute observers of American ways."

—DIANE JOHNSON

"Francine Prose has a wickedly sharp ear . . . and no telling detail escapes her observation."

—*New York Times Book Review*

"Hilarious and shocking. . . . Prose [is] one of the best and quirkiest fiction writers."

—*San Francisco Chronicle*

"Ms. Prose's novels are powerful precisely because of the way the buried seriousness infuses and transforms works that nonetheless remain comic in their intent and effect."

—*New York Observer*

"One of our finest writers."

—LARRY MCMURTRY

Marion Ettlinger

About the Author

FRANCINE PROSE is the author of many ac-
claimed works of fiction, including *A Changed
Man*; *Blue Angel*, a finalist for the National
Book Award; *Guided Tours of Hell*; *Primitive
People*; *Women and Children First*; and *House-
hold Saints*. Her nonfiction books include *The
Lives of the Muses* and the forthcoming *Car-
avaggio*. A recipient of numerous grants and
awards, including Guggenheim and Fulbright
Fellowships, she was a Director's Fellow at the
Center for Scholars and Writers at the New
York Public Library. She lives in New York
City.

The Peaceable Kingdom

THE
PEACEABLE
KINGDOM

stories

FRANCINE
PROSE

Perennial
An Imprint of HarperCollins*Publishers*

The following stories appeared, in slightly different form, in these publications: "Talking Dog" in *The Yale Review*; "Cauliflower Heads" in *The Michigan Quarterly Review*; "Rubber Life" in *The North American Review* and *The Pushcart Prize XVII*; "Amazing" in *TriQuarterly*; "Ghirlandaio" in *Tikkun* and *The Tikkun Anthology*; "Amateur Voodoo" in *Boulevard* and *The Sophisticated Cat*; "Potato World" in *Boulevard*; "Dog Stories" in *Special Report* and *The Best American Short Stories 1991*; "Imaginary Problems" in *Antaeus*; "The Shining Path" in *The Indiana Review*.

A hardcover edition of this book was published in 1993 by Farrar, Straus and Giroux. It is here reprinted by arrangement with Farrar, Straus and Giroux.

HarperCollins books may be purchased for educational, business, or sales promotional use. For information please write: Special Markets Department, HarperCollins Publishers, 10 East 53rd Street, New York, NY 10022.

First Perennial edition published 2005.

Designed by Cynthia Krupat

Library of Congress Cataloging-in-Publication Data

Prose, Francine.
    The peaceable kingdom : stories / Francine Prose.— 1st Perennial ed.
      p. cm.
    Contents: Talking dog—Cauliflower heads—Rubber life—Amazing—Ghirlandaio—Amateur voodoo—Potato world—Dog stories—Imaginary problems—The shining path—Hansel and Gretel.
    ISBN 0-06-075404-4
      I. Title.

PS3566.R68P4 2005
513'.54—dc22

                                        2005042956

05 06 07 08 09 PENN/RRD 10 9 8 7 6 5 4 3 2 1

Contents

The Peaceable Kingdom

TALKING
DOG

THE DOG WAS GOING to Florida. The dog knew all the best sleeping places along the side of the highway, and if my sister wanted to come along, the dog would be glad to pace himself so my sister could keep up. My sister told our family this when she came back to the dinner table from which Mother and I had watched her kneeling in the snowy garden, crouched beside the large shaggy white dog, her ear against its mouth.

My sister's chair faced the window, and when the dog first appeared in our yard, she'd said, "Oh, I know that dog," and jumped up and ran out the door. I thought she'd meant whose dog it was, not that she knew it to talk to.

"What dog?" My father slowly turned his head.

"A dog, dear," Mother said.

That year it came as a great surprise how many sad things could happen at once. At first you might think the odds are that one grief might exempt you, but that year I learned the odds are that nothing can keep you safe. So many concurrent painful events altered our sense of each one, just as a color appears to change when another color is placed beside it.

That year my father was going blind from a disease of the retina, a condition we knew a lot about because my father was a scientist and used to lecture us on it at dinner with the glittery detached fascination he'd once had for research gossip and new developments in the lab. Yet as his condition worsened he'd stopped talking about it; he could still read but had trouble with stairs and had begun to touch the furniture. Out in daylight he needed special glasses, like twin tiny antique cameras, and he ducked his head as he put them on, as if burrowing under a cloth. I was ashamed for anyone to see and ashamed of being embarrassed.

My father still consulted part-time for a lab that used dogs in experiments, and at night he worked at home with a microscope and a tape recorder. "Slide 109," he'd say. "Liver condition normal." My sister had always loved animals, but no one yet saw a connection between my father dissecting dogs and my sister talking to them.

For several weeks before that night when the white dog came through our yard, my sister lay in bed with the curtains drawn and got up only at mealtime. Mother told the high school that my sister had bronchitis. At first my sister's friends telephoned, but only one, Marcy, still called. I'd hear Mother telling Marcy that my sister was much better, being friendlier to Marcy than she'd ever been before. Marcy had cracked a girl's front tooth and been sent to a special school. Each time Marcy telephoned, Mother called my sister's name and, when she didn't answer, said she must be sleeping. I believed my sister was faking it but even I'd begun to have the sickish, panicky feeling you get when someone playing dead takes too long getting up.

One night at dinner my sister told us that every culture but ours believed that ordinary household pets were the messengers of the dead.

"I don't know about that," my father said. "I don't know about *every* culture."

After that it was just a matter of time till she met the dog with a message. And we all knew who it was that my sister was waiting to hear from.

Her boyfriend, Jimmy Kowalchuk, had just been killed in Vietnam.

Mother had gone with my sister to Jimmy Kowalchuk's funeral. I was not allowed to attend, though I'd been in love with him, too. All day in school all I could think of was how many hours, how many minutes till they lowered him in the ground. It was a little like the time they executed Caryl Chessman and the whole school counted down the minutes till he died. The difference was that with Jimmy I was the only one counting, and I had to keep reminding myself that he was already dead.

Mother came home from the funeral in a bubbly, talkative mood. After my sister drifted off, Mother sat on the arm of my father's chair. She said, "They call this country a melting pot but if you ask me there's still a few lumps. Believe it or not, they had two priests—one Polish and one Puerto Rican. The minute I saw them I said to myself: This will take twice as long."

Mother had never liked it that Jimmy was half Polish, half Puerto Rican—if he couldn't be white Protestant, better Puerto Rican completely. She never liked it that our family knew someone named Jimmy Kowalchuk, and she liked it least of all that we knew someone fighting in Vietnam. Every Wednesday night Mother counseled draft resisters, and it made her livid that Jimmy had volunteered.

"Guess what?" Mother told us. "His name wasn't even Jimmy. It was Hymie. That's what the priests and the relatives kept saying. Hymie. Hymie. Hymie. Do you think she would have gone out with him if she had known that?"

"J pronounced Y," my father said. "J-A-I-M-E."

"Pedant," mumbled Mother, so softly only I heard.

"Excuse me?" my father said.

"Nothing," Mother said. "Maybe we should have got her that pony she nagged us about in junior high. Maybe we should have let her keep that falcon that needed a home."

To me she said, "This does not mean you, dear. You cannot have a bird or a pony."

But I didn't want a bird or a pony. I still wanted Jimmy Kowalchuk. And I alone knew that he and my sister had had a great love, a tragic love. For unlike my parents I had seen what Jimmy had gone through to win it.

The first time was on a wet gray day, winter twilight, after school. My parents were in the city, seeing one of my father's doctors, my sister was taking care of me, we were supposed to stay home. Jimmy came to take my sister out in his lemon-yellow '65 Malibu. My sister must have decided it was safer to bring me along—better an accomplice than a potential snitch. I felt like a criminal, like the Barrow Gang on the Jericho Turnpike, ready to hit the floor if I saw Mother's car in the opposite lane.

As Jimmy left the highway for smaller and smaller

roads, I felt safer from my parents but more nervous about Jimmy. He was slight and tense and Latin with a wispy beard, dangerous and pretty, like Jesus with an earring. We drove past black trees, marshy scrub-pine lots, perfect for dumping bodies, not far from a famous spot where the Mafia often did. The light was fading and scraps of fog clung regretfully to the windshield.

Jimmy pulled off on the side of the road beside the bank of a frozen lake. "Ladies," he said, "I'll have to ask you to step outside for a minute." Leaning across my sister, he opened the door on her side and then arched back over the seat and opened mine for me.

A wet mist prickled our faces—tiny sharp needles of ice.

"I'm freezing," said my sister.

I said, "Do you think he'd leave us here?"

She said, "Stupid, why would my boyfriend leave us in the middle of nowhere?" I hadn't known for certain till then that Jimmy was her boyfriend. He hadn't even touched her leg when he'd reached down to shift gears.

Jimmy rammed the car in gear and pointed it at the lake and sped out onto the ice and hit the brake and spun. It was thrilling and terrifying to see a car whip around like a snake, and there was also a grace in it, the weightless skimming of a skater. The yellow car gathered the last of the light and cast a faint lemon glow on the ice.

Suddenly we heard the ice crack—first with a squeak, then a groan. My sister grabbed my upper arm and dug her fingers in.

Jimmy must have heard it, too, because the car glided

to a stop and he gingerly turned it around and drove back in our direction. I stood up on tiptoe though I could see perfectly well. Then I looked at my sister as if she knew what was going to happen.

I was shocked by my sister's expression: not a trace of fear or concern, but an unreadable concentration and the sullen fixed anger I saw sometimes when we fought. She was very careful not to look like that out in the world, except if she saw a pet she thought was being mistreated. It was like watching a simmering pot, lid rattling, about to boil over, but her lids were halfway down and you couldn't see what was cooking. At the moment I understood that men would always like her better, prefer her smoky opacity to a transparent face like mine.

On the drive home Jimmy elaborated on his theory of danger. He said it was important for males to regularly test themselves against potentially fatal risks. He said it was like a checkup or maybe a vacation—you did it regularly for your health and for a hit on how you were doing.

"That's bullshit," my sister said.

"She thinks it's bullshit," Jimmy told me. "Do you think it's bullshit, kid?"

I knew he was inviting me to contradict my sister; it made me feel like a younger brother instead of an eighth-grade girl. I knew that if I agreed with him I might get to come along again. But that wasn't my reason for saying no. At that moment I believed him.

"The kid knows," Jimmy said, and I whispered: The kid. The kid. The kid.

"This danger thing," Jimmy told us, "is only about yourself. It would be criminal to take chances with somebody else's life. I would never go over the speed limit with you ladies in the car." I hunched my shoulders and burrowed into the fragrant back seat. I felt—and I think my sister felt—supremely taken care of.

My parents were often in the city with my father's doctors, occasionally staying over for tests, not returning till the next day. They told my sister to take care of me, though I didn't need taking care of.

Jimmy would drive over when he got through at Babylon Roofing and Siding. He loved his job and sometimes stopped to show us roofs he'd done. His plan was to have his own company and retire to Florida young and get a little house with grapefruit and mango trees in the yard. He said this to my sister. He wanted her to want it, too.

My sister said, "Mangoes in Florida? You're thinking about Puerto Rico."

One night Jimmy parked in front of a furniture store and told us to slouch down and keep our eye on the dark front window. My sister and I were alone for so long I began to get frightened.

A light flickered on inside the store, the flame from Jimmy's lighter, bright enough to see Jimmy smiling and waving, reclining in a lounger.

When Jimmy talked about testing himself, he said he did it sometimes, but I began to wonder if he thought about it always. Just sitting in a diner, waiting for his coffee, he'd take the pointiest knife he could find and dance it between his fingers. I wondered what our role in it was. I wondered if he and my sister were playing a game of chicken: all she had to do was cry "Stop!" and Jimmy would have won. Once he ate a cigarette filter. Once he jumped off a building.

One evening Jimmy drove me and my sister over to his apartment. He lived in a basement apartment of a brick private house. It struck me as extraordinary: people lived in basement apartments. But it wasn't a shock to my sister, who knew where everything was and confidently got two beers from Jimmy's refrigerator.

Jimmy turned on the six o'clock news and the three of us sat on his bed. There was the usual Vietnam report: helicopters, gunfire. A sequence showed American troops filing through the jungle. The camera moved in for a close-up of the soldiers' faces, faces that I recognize now as the faces of frightened boys but that I mistook then for cruel grown men, happy in what they were doing.

My sister said, "Wow. Any one of those suckers could just get blown off that trail." On her face was that combustible mix of sympathy and smoldering anger, and in her voice rage and contempt combined with admiration. I could tell Jimmy was jealous that she looked like that because of the soldiers, and he desperately wanted her to look that way for him. I knew, even if he didn't, that she already had, and that she looked like that if she saw a dog in a parked car, in the heat.

Jimmy had a high draft number but he went down and enlisted. He said he couldn't sit back and let other men do the dying, an argument I secretly thought was crazy and brave and terrific. Mother said it was ridiculous, no one had to die, every kid she counseled wound up with a psychiatric 1-Y. And when Jimmy died she seemed confirmed; he had proved her right.

On the night of the funeral, Mother told us how Jimmy died. The friend who'd accompanied his body home had given a little speech. He said often at night Jimmy sneaked out to where they weren't supposed to be; once a flare went off and they saw him freaking around in the jungle. He said they felt better knowing that crazy Kowalchuk was out there fucking around.

Mother said, "That's what he said at the service. 'Out there fucking around.' "

But I was too hurt to listen, I was feeling so stupid for having imagined that Jimmy's stunts were about my sister and me.

Mother said, "Of course I think it's terrible that the boy got killed. But I have to say I don't hate it that now the two of them can't get married."

After that it was just a matter of time till my sister met the white dog that Jimmy had sent from the other world to take her to Florida.

My sister didn't go to Florida, or anyway not yet. Eventually she recovered—recovered or stopped pretending. Every night after dinner Mother said, "She's eating well. She's improving." Talking to strange dogs in the yard was apparently not a problem. Father's problem was a real problem; my sister's would improve. I knew that Mother felt this way, and once more she was right.

One night Marcy telephoned, Mother called my sister, and my sister came out of her room. She took the phone and told Marcy, "Sure, great. See you. Bye."

"Marcy knows about a party," she said.

Mother said, "Wonderful, dear," though in the past there were always fights about going to parties with Marcy.

We all stayed up till my sister came home, though we all pretended to sleep. My window was over the front door and I watched her on the front step, struggling to unlock the door, holding something bulky pressed against her belly. At last she disappeared inside. Something hit the floor with a thud. I heard my sister running. There was so much commotion we all felt justified rushing downstairs. Mother helped my father down, they came along rather quickly.

We found my sister in the kitchen. It was quiet and very dark. The refrigerator was open, not for food but for light. Bathed in its glow, my sister was rhythmically stroking a large iguana that stood poised, alert, its head slightly raised, on the butcher block by the stove.

In the equalizing darkness my father saw almost as well as we did. "Jesus Christ," he said.

My sister said, "He was a little freaked. You can try turning the light on."

Only then did we notice that the lizard's foot was bandaged. My sister said, "This drunken jerk bit off one of his toes. He got all the guys at the party to bet that he wouldn't do it. I just waded in and took the poor thing and the guy just gave it up. The asshole couldn't have cared very much if he was going to bite its toes off."

"Watch your language," Mother said. "What a cruel thing to do! Is this the kind of teenager you're going to parties with?"

"Animals," my father said. After that there was a silence, during which all of us thought that once my father would have unwrapped the bandage and taken a look at that foot.

"His name's Reynaldo," my sister said.

"Sounds Puerto Rican," said Mother.

Once there would have been a fight about her keeping the iguana, but like some brilliant general, my sister had retreated and recouped and emerged from her bedroom, victorious and in control. At that moment I hated her for always getting her way, for always outlasting everyone and being so weird and dramatic and never letting you know for sure what was real and what she was faking.

Reynaldo had the run of my sister's room, no one dared open the door. After school she'd lie belly down on her bed, cheek to cheek with Reynaldo. And in a way it was lucky that my father couldn't see that.

One night the phone rang. Mother covered the receiver and said, "Thank you, Lord. It's a boy."

It was a boy who had been at the party and seen my sister rescue Reynaldo. His name was Greg; he was a college student, studying for a business degree.

After he and my sister went out a few times, Mother invited Greg to dinner. I ate roast beef and watched him charm everyone but me. He described my sister grabbing the iguana out of its torturer's hands. He said, "When I saw her do that, I thought, This is someone I want to know better." He and my parents talked about her like some distant mutual friend. I stared hard at my sister, wanting her to miss Jimmy, too, but she was playing with her food, I couldn't tell what she was thinking.

Greg had a widowed mother and two younger sisters; he'd gotten out of the draft by being their sole support. He said he wouldn't go anyway, he'd go to Canada first. No one mentioned Reynaldo, though we could hear him scrabbling jealously around my sister's room.

Reynaldo wasn't invited on their dates and neither, obviously, was I. I knew Greg didn't drive onto the ice or break into furniture stores. He took my sister to Godard movies and told us how much she liked them.

One Saturday my sister and Greg took Reynaldo out for a drive. And when they returned—I waited up—the iguana wasn't with them.

"Where's Reynaldo?" I asked.

"A really nice pet shop," she said. And then for the first time I understood that Jimmy was really dead.

Not long after that my father died. His doctors had made a mistake. It was not a disease of the retina but a tumor of the brain. You'd think they would have known that, checked for that right away, but he was a scientist, they saw themselves in him and didn't want to know. Before he died he disappeared, one piece at a time. My sister and I slowly turned away so as not to see what was missing.

Greg was very helpful throughout this terrible time. Six months after my father died, Greg and my sister got married. By then he'd graduated and got a marketing job with a potato-chip company. Mother and I lived alone in the house—as we'd had, really, for some time. My father and sister had left so gradually that the door hardly swung shut behind them. Father's Buick sat in the garage, as it had since he'd lost his vision, and every time we saw it we thought about all that had happened.

My sister and Greg bought a house nearby; sometimes Mother and I went for dinner. Greg told us about his work and the interesting things he found out. In the Northeast they liked the burnt chips, the lumpy mis-shapen ones, but down South every chip had to be pale and thin and perfect.

"A racial thing, no doubt," I said, but no one seemed to hear, though one of Mother's favorite subjects was race relations down South. I'd thought my sister might laugh or get angry, but she was a different person. A slower, solid, heavier person who was eating a lot of chips.

One afternoon the doorbell rang, and it was Jimmy Kowalchuk. It took me a while to recognize him; he didn't have his beard. For a second—just a second—I was afraid to open the door. He was otherwise unchanged except that he'd got even thinner, and looked even less Polish and even more Puerto Rican.

He was wearing army fatigues. I was glad Mother wasn't home. He gave me a hug, my first ever from him, and lifted me off the ground. He said no, he was never dead, never even missing.

He said, "Some army computer glitch, some creep's clerical error." My father's death had made it easier to believe that people made such mistakes, and for one dizzying moment I allowed myself to imagine that maybe Jimmy's being alive meant my father was, too.

"You got older," Jimmy said. "This is like *The Twilight Zone*." And he must have thought so—that time had stopped in his absence. I invited him in, made him sit down, and then told him about my sister.

Jimmy got up and left the house. He didn't ask whom she'd married. He didn't ask where they lived, though I knew he was going to find her.

Once again I waited, counting down the hours. This time, although weeks passed, it was like counting one two three. Four—the phone rang. It was Greg. He had come home from the office and found my sister packed and gone.

A week later my sister called collect from St. Petersburg, Florida. She said Jimmy knew a guy, a buddy from Vietnam, he had found Jimmy a rental house and a job with a roofing company. They had hurricanes down there that would rip the top of your house off. She emphasized the hurricane part, as if that made it all make sense. In fact, she seemed so sure about the sensibleness of her situation that she made me promise to tell Mother and Greg she'd called and that she was fine.

Mother had less trouble believing that my sister had been kidnapped than that she'd left Greg and taken off with her dead boyfriend from Vietnam. It was a lot to process at once; she'd seen Jimmy buried. Greg had never heard of Jimmy, which made me wonder about my sister. I thought about Reynaldo, how forcefully she had seized him, how easily she'd let him go.

My sister had called from a pay phone. All she'd said was "St. Petersburg." Mother telephoned Mrs. Kowalchuk and got Jimmy's address from her. Afterwards Mother said, "The woman thinks it's a miracle. The army loses her son, she goes through hell, and she thinks it's the will of God."

Mother wrote my sister a letter. A month passed. There was no answer. By now Greg was in permanent shock, though he still went to work. One night he told us about a dipless chip now in the blueprint stage. Then even Mother knew we were alone, and her eyes filled with tears. She said, "Florida! It's warm there. When is your Easter vacation?"

We took my father's Buick, a decision that almost convinced us that some reason besides paralysis explained its still being in our garage. I sat up front beside Mother, scrunched low in the spongy seat. States went by. The highway was always the same. There was nothing to watch except Mother, staring furiously at the road. Though the temperature rose steadily, Mother wouldn't turn off the heat and by Florida I was riding with my head out the window, for air, and also working on a tan for Jimmy.

It was easy finding the address we got from Mrs. Kowalchuk. They were living in a shack, but newly painted white, and with stubby marigolds lining the cracked front walk.

"Tobacco Road," said Mother.

Then Mother and I saw Jimmy working out in the yard. His back was smooth and golden and muscles churned under his skin as he swayed from side to side, planing something—a door. Behind him a tree with shiny leaves sagged under its great weight of grapefruit, and sunlight dappled the round yellow fruit and the down on Jimmy's shoulders.

Jimmy stopped working and turned and smiled. He didn't seem surprised to see us. As he came toward us a large dog roused itself from the ground at his feet, a long-haired white dog so much like the one my sister spoke to in our yard that for a moment I felt faint and had to lean on Mother.

Mother shook me off. She hardly noticed the dog. She was advancing on Jimmy.

"I wasn't dead, it was a mistake." Jimmy sounded apologetic.

"Obviously," said Mother. Then she told me not to move and went into the house.

I couldn't have moved if I'd wanted. Every muscle had fused, every tiny flutter and tic felt grossly magnified and disgusting. I had never seen Jimmy without a shirt. I wanted to touch his back. He said, "I got my grapefruit tree."

"Obviously," I said in Mother's voice, and Jimmy grinned and we laughed. On the table lay a pile of tools. He wasn't stabbing them between his fingers. He must have gotten that out of his system, dying and coming back.

Even though it was Jimmy's house, we felt we couldn't go in. Every inch of space was taken up by what my mother and sister were saying. Where was Jimmy's Malibu? We walked to a cafeteria and stood in a line of elderly couples deciding between the baked fish and the chicken. Jimmy couldn't be served there, he wasn't wearing a shirt. The manager was sorry, it was a Florida law. Jimmy had gone to Vietnam and been lost in a computer and now couldn't even get a cup of cafeteria coffee. But I couldn't say that, my head was ringing with things I couldn't say—for example, that I had waited for him, and my sister hadn't.

Half a block from Jimmy's house, we saw an upsetting sight—my mother and sister in Mother's car with the engine running.

"Going for lunch?" Jimmy said. But we all knew they weren't.

Mother told me to get in back. Jimmy looked in and I saw him notice my sister's suitcase. He did nothing to stop us—that was the strangest part. He let me get in and let us take off and stood there and watched us go.

I never knew, I never found out what Mother said to

my sister. Or maybe it wasn't what Mother said, perhaps it was all about Jimmy. Once again I thought of Reynaldo and my sister's giving him up. If I never knew what had happened with that, how could I ask about Jimmy? You assume you will ask the important questions, you will get to them sooner or later, an idea that ignores two things: the power of shyness, the fact of death.

That should have been the last time I saw Jimmy Kowalchuk—a wounded young god glowing with sun in a firmament of grapefruit. But there was one more time, nearer home, in the dead of winter.

Before that, Greg took my sister back. They went on as if nothing had happened. Greg got a promotion. They moved to a nicer house. I saw my sister sometimes. Jimmy was not a subject. I never asked about him, his name never came up. I would talk about school sometimes, but she never seemed to be listening. Once she said, out of nowhere, "I guess people want different things at different times in their lives."

I was a senior in high school when my sister was killed. Her car jumped a divider on the Sunrise Highway. It was a new car Greg kept well maintained, so it was nobody's fault.

On the way to the funeral Mother sat between me and Greg. When my sister went back to Greg, Mother had gone back to him, too. But that day, in the funeral car, she was talking to me.

"What was I doing?" Mother said. "I knew I couldn't make you girls happy. I was just trying to give you the chance to be happy if you wanted. I thought that life was a corridor with doors that opened and shut as you passed, and I was just trying to keep them from slamming on you."

The reality of my sister's death hadn't come home to me yet, and though my father's dying had taught me that death was final, perhaps Jimmy's reappearance had put that in some doubt. Guiltily I wondered if Jimmy would be at my sister's funeral, as if it were a party at which he might show up.

Jimmy came with his mother, a tiny woman in black. He was gritty, unshaven, tragically handsome in a wrinkled suit and dark glasses. He looked as if he'd hitchhiked or rode up on the Greyhound.

I went and stood beside Jimmy. No one expected that. After the service I left with him. Not even I could believe it. All the relatives watched me leave, Mother and Greg and my sister's friend Marcy. I wondered if this was how Jimmy felt, driving out onto the ice.

Jimmy was driving a cousin's rusted Chevy Nova. We dropped his mother at her house. Jimmy and I kept going. I could tell he'd been drinking. He must have given up on his rule about endangering other people. Finally I was alone with him, but it wasn't what I'd pictured. I wondered which friend I could call if I needed someone to pick me up.

I was starting college in the fall. I had some place I had to be. A new life was expecting me with its eye on the clock and no time and no patience for me to run away with Jimmy.

Jimmy drove to a crowded strip somewhere off Hempstead Turnpike. We stopped at the Shamrock, a dark, beery-smelling bar. Jimmy and I sat at a table. The bartender took our order. The regulars seemed too relaxed to pay any special attention to a Charlie Mansonesque Puerto Rican and a girl, below the drinking age, nervously sipping her beer.

Jimmy put away several boilermakers. He was getting drunker and drunker. He kept talking about my sister. He said some very unlikely things but nothing too strange to believe, especially when he repeated it, each time exactly the same.

He told me that the white dog had shown up the first day they moved to Florida. It ran up to my sister in the yard; they seemed to know each other. The dog, said my sister, had come to her after Jimmy died and personally guaranteed it that Jimmy was still alive. Jimmy said, "I had to wonder how the goddamn dog found out our Florida address."

The light in the Shamrock was fading. Jimmy blamed the war. He said, "*I* died and got through it halfway all right. But it gets you no matter what. I came back but it was too late. Your sister was talking to dogs."

I pictured Mother setting out silver platters of roast beef for the relatives who would be coming back after the funeral. I saw light wink off her coffee urn and the plates of little iced cakes and for one shaming moment a bright bubble shone and popped in the dusty fermented air of the bar.

It hadn't scared Mother but it had scared Jimmy, my sister talking to dogs. I remembered how unresistingly

Jimmy had let Mother take her, as easily as my sister had let Reynaldo go. I had a vision of people pulling at each other, and of the people who loved them letting them slip through their hands and almost liking the silky feel of them sliding through their fingers.

Jimmy said my sister blamed herself for my father's death. She'd told Jimmy that when she realized he was looking at slides of dead dogs, she wished for something to happen so he would have to stop it. No matter how much my father told us about his disease, my sister believed that somehow she had caused it, and she had this pet iguana that was the only one she could tell. She told Jimmy the iguana had died in her arms and she blamed herself for that, too.

Tears welled up in Jimmy's eyes. He said, "The woman had powers."

For a fraction of a second I thought I might still want him. But I didn't want him. I just didn't want her to have him forever. I was shocked to be so jealous when death meant it could never be fixed. I didn't want it to be that way, but that was how it was.

I wanted to tell Jimmy that my sister didn't have powers. I wanted to say that her only power was the power to make everyone look, she'd had nothing, nothing to do with my father going blind, and she had lied to one of us about what happened to that iguana. I wanted to say she'd lied to us all, she'd faked it about the dog, as if it mattered whether the animal spoke, as if love were about the truth, as if he would love her less—and not more—for pretending to talk to a dog.

CAULIFLOWER
HEADS

EUROPE WAS CRAWLING with adulterous couples. Mostly, for some reason, one saw them at ruins, respectfully tripping over the archaeological rubble. Just like regular tourists they seemed to be under some terrible strain, but unlike regular tourists they hardly looked at anything, so that when, say, a lizard streaked across their path they'd jump and fall into each other with apologetic smiles, more like awkward teenagers than adults risking the forbidden.

In the ruins of Herculaneum, Susanna saw the quintessential adulterous couple leaving one of the underground rooms just as she and Jerry were entering. The couple started as if they'd been caught embracing, as if they often met in the cave-like room and were shocked to see anyone else. They looked vaguely Eastern European—raincoats in the summer heat and frumpy business suits. The woman was pretty, in a frizzy way, with oddly colorless eyes and hair. She carried a leather briefcase and wore sensible, mannish shoes. The man was tall and also had colorless hair combed to cover a bald spot.

Later, when Susanna and Jerry stopped at a trattoria down the road, the couple were eating lunch there, or rather chain-smoking through it. A haze hovered over the plates of food they ordered and didn't touch. Once, when the woman lit up a smoke, her lover pushed back her sleeve and pressed his cheek to the inside of her forearm.

Watching, Susanna felt something inside her chest go

soggy and expansive, like that trick when you pleat a drinking-straw wrapper and then drip water on it. Across the table Jerry was happily tucking away his penne al'amatriciana. Jerry and Susanna had only been married three weeks. Susanna wondered: Wasn't one's honeymoon cruelly early to be envying the adulterous?

Of course she couldn't ask Jerry. *That* would have been cruel, and even if he managed not to take it personally, he'd think she was silly for worrying about this when the planet was dying.

When Jerry saw a lizard in the ruins he took a picture of it. He was very aware of how many species were disappearing. If he and Susanna ever had children, he wanted to show them animals that by then might no longer exist. Susanna couldn't picture the children she and Jerry might have, and certainly not a cozy scene around the lamplit kitchen table: Jerry showing the children photos of vanished animal life.

And yet Jerry's hobby—elegiac nature photography—had deeply moved Susanna when they first fell in love. They'd met when Jerry came to speak at Susanna's college; Jerry lived near the college and was brought in at the last minute after the scheduled speaker, a former cabinet member, tried to get off a plane in mid-flight when the movie ended.

Jerry was a consultant on radioactive waste disposal. When your town dump glowed in the dark, your mayor called Jerry. Jerry gave Susanna's class the global bad news with such deep personal grief that she was overcome with longing to protect him from what he knew. He told them to look to the right, then the left, and imagine the people on both sides with giant green cauliflower heads. Then he said they were kidding themselves, because this would never happen; they would not evolve into toxic creatures capable of thriving on environmental poisons. They would die and the earth would die and turn into a radioactive desert glowing in the sunless sky. Then the college students were filled with shame for having imagined that they could be saved.

Jerry had said, "It's up to your generation to make sure it doesn't happen." And Susanna had thought: Well, obviously. Jerry would show her how.

Perhaps this was the reason their courtship was so intense: it was as if the bomb had dropped and they had fifteen minutes to live. All through Susanna's last semester they met in a dark bar near campus where married professors met girl students, though Jerry was single and didn't teach, so really there was no need.

Susanna had forgotten to think about her future beyond graduation, which made it easier, when school ended, to move from the dorm to Jerry's house. On summer evenings they frequented the same dark bar near campus. The girls had gone off to glamorous internships, the professors home to their families and the books they'd been meaning to write. Leaning so close their heads touched, Jerry told Susanna stories: twice his office had been burglarized and strategic files stolen. In July he heard some hopeful news and gripped her hand till it hurt: some PCB-eating macrophage had looked good in the lab.

But after they'd lived together that winter he seemed to forget about her saving the world, and even that she was in it, so that often he seemed surprised and pleased to find her in his house. Susanna tried to see this as a positive sign. Perhaps if he overestimated the chance of her vanishing from his life he might also be mistaken about the ozone layer. She herself was worried about the future of the planet and so felt petty and ashamed when the subject began to seem like an annoying tic of Jerry's. If you took pleasure in a sunny day, he brought up global warming. Several times she'd caught herself on the edge of saying that she would rather the world end than have to think about it all the time.

But anyone could see that Jerry was right. That spring a toxic dump site turned up in their back yard; well, not actually their back yard—two or three miles down the road. Susanna and Jerry stood on a bluff overlooking the devastation. Acres of muddy bulldozer tracks, glittery patches of broken glass, strips of bloody gauze unfurled like a vampire fraternity prank.

Jerry cleared his throat and said, "Probably we should get married."

It bothered Susanna a little—proposed to at a dump site!—but she told herself it was perfect: the marriage of the future. At once dedicated and resigned, she had told Jerry yes.

———

So they had come to Italy, combining their honeymoon with the world ecology conference in Milan, to which Jerry had been invited to give a brief address. They landed in Rome and rented a car and drove south to Pompeii and Herculaneum, where, as Susanna watched the adulterous couple cannibalizing each other at the next table, Jerry washed down his pasta with wine and said, "What amazes me is how people can go to these ruins and not take it personally. I mean, no one who died here or at Pompeii thought the big one was going to hit. It was just business as usual, reading the paper, baking bread . . . bingo. You're history. These tourists trip through, acting like it's someone else's problem, and it never crosses their mind that they're looking at Main Street a hundred years from now."

Susanna said, "Jerry, give them a break. They're tourists on vacation." Sometimes she felt it was mean of him to want people to think like he did.

But why was the adulterous couple so tense and distracted and silent? Susanna wondered what they had left behind and how much time they had. She thought of the lovers of Pompeii, killed in each other's arms. The lovers of Pompeii were charred to ash, the Herculaneans covered with mud.

"Vacation!" Jerry snorted. "They should see what *I* see." He meant the statistics that crossed his desk: wildly alarming health reports and grim projections into the future. Susanna thought of paintings of St. Jerome with a human skull on his desk; most likely the saints of the future would have printouts instead of skulls. But would there be saints in the future, and who would paint their portraits to hang in the museums when there were no people left to go to museums and see them?

The farther north they traveled, the better Susanna liked it. She was glad when they left the South, where the dust and heat made everything shimmer ambiguously, like in spaghetti Westerns that don't care if you follow the plot. She was happiest in Umbria and the spookier parts of Tuscany, where you felt the romance these people craved was not the romance of love but the romance of poisoning each other with undetectable toxins. She particularly liked Gubbio: so stony, so unforgiving. You could wait out the apocalypse in one of its thick-walled palaces; there your life would be hard and clean with no disturbing soft spots.

At first Jerry trailed Susanna up the steep cobbled streets, panting and making coronary jokes. But soon he was talking about how life here whipped you into shape: no wonder the old ladies had such terrific calves. Sometimes Susanna hung back and let him pull her uphill, but at the church doors she broke away and hurried in ahead. She didn't like to watch him paging through his Michelin Guide, entering the churches with his head in a book. He approached each cathedral like a research problem; once she saw him peering into an empty confessional.

In Florence, at San Lorenzo, before an altar painting

of saints, a British child was asking her parents how the different martyrs died. "That's all she wants to know," her father said to Susanna. "What happened to the poor blokes."

Jerry pointed to the tray of eyeballs that St. Lucy was carrying. "Know what those are?" he asked the girl. "Marbles," he answered for her, and the adults giggled nervously.

Jerry had no patience with martyrs; he said they were deluded and psychotically self-indulgent. He said, "Life is short enough without asking someone to shorten it for you." His favorite frescoes were of people engaged in ordinary tasks, oblivious to the big moment: fishermen angling peacefully in the Red Sea while Pharaoh's soldiers are drowning; gamblers dicing in the shadow of the Crucifixion. For Jerry, these had the relevance of the latest news—just transpose the sailors in the sea to the otters in the oil spill. And in fact, like so much of the news, these paintings made Susanna feel guilty.

She was starting to feel guilty a lot—guilty for being a tourist. How she envied the travelers who fought for their sightseeing pleasure against the fear of missing something and some greater unnamed dread. She even envied the retirees who knew they deserved a vacation. Was that more or less pathetic than envying the adulterous? Jerry said the best cure for guilt was taking positive action, but it was hard, in foreign towns, knowing what action to take. And really, had she ever? She'd known to go up and ask Jerry for a copy of his speech, but she was no longer sure that seducing him was a step toward saving the world.

There was a new thing Jerry liked in bed: pinning her hands above her head. It made her feel like St. Sebastian waiting for the arrows. Jerry was polite about it. Before he did it he stopped and smiled, embarrassed, asking permission. He didn't take criticism well, he got quite pouty and sulky, so Susanna didn't mention that it wasn't her favorite thing. She just went passive, thinking, I'm the Gandhi of the bedroom, and feeling guilty for thinking of Gandhi in this debasing context. Gandhi was her hero; she and Jerry had that in common.

Her parents had feared that her worshipping Gandhi might be a warning sign of anorexia, though it should have been obvious how much she liked food. Jerry worried the opposite; sometimes he dissuaded her from a second helping of pasta. He encouraged her to wear clothes that showed off her skinny body, miniskirts and halters in which she looked about twelve. He especially approved of her dressing like that for his colleagues. She knew she was a trophy to him and felt guilty for liking that, too.

She also liked it and also felt guilty when they got to Milan and checked into the hotel where the conference was being held, and at the first night's dinner-dance Jerry steered her through the room, and she felt her blond hair and tiny white dress dazzling the famous ecologists. On the street, with Italian girls around, she didn't feel so dazzling—but most of the ecologists were middle-aged

men, even older than Jerry. For them she was all youth
and sex rolled up in one female body. This reassured her
in a way she'd missed since she and Jerry met. She knew
it was unliberated if what you were doing for the planet
was making ecologists happy with fleeting moments of
fantasy sex. But wasn't even that better than doing nothing
at all?

It was easy to feel pretty in the hotel dining room, amid
the black enamel and chrome and pots of swollen white
lilies. She and Jerry sat down and couldn't very well get
up when they found themselves sharing a table with three
Politburo members. In fact, they were Bulgarian, or so
their name cards said. They nodded at Jerry and Susanna
and then stared grimly ahead. Sometimes they whispered
to each other. Susanna thought of the couple at Herculaneum. Had she mistaken Eastern European social
style for some special intensity?

All the waiters looked like male models with designer
white jackets. Serving, they brushed suspiciously close to
Susanna's bare arms, and the space around her felt
charged, a pleasing distraction from the strain of dining
with Bulgarians. The dance band, five Malaysian kids,
played a kind of modified swing. Susanna pulled Jerry
out on the floor, where she pressed herself against him
and spread her legs and bent her knees so her skirt rode
up on her hips. Jerry jitterbugged well enough, and as
he twirled her around, she threw back her head and closed
her eyes and felt the eyes of the ecologists warming her
arms and legs.

———

Outside the conference room they picked up earphones for simultaneous translation. The first speaker was a professor from the University of Milan, who welcomed the participants and expressed his hope that together they could solve their common problems and that this year, unlike last, the discourse would not bog down in petty nationalist grievances. The current crisis was everyone's fault, no one country's more than the rest.

One by one the ecologists made their way to the podium. Each spoke for ten minutes and took questions from the floor. Everyone chain-smoked feverishly in the audience and on stage; after every few speeches they took a coffee break and chain-smoked in the hall. Several of the speakers reported on particular rivers or mountains or forests. Meditating on the depletion of the earth's resources had lined their faces and made them look brooding, unacademic, and Yves Montandish. The Europeans talked slowly and out of the sides of their mouths. The Americans were stiffer, more boyish, and, like Jerry, more nervous.

Jerry's speech was too close to lunch and did not go well. It was very different from what he'd told Susanna's class. Perhaps he should have asked them to look to both sides and imagine their colleagues with cauliflower heads. Instead, he dimmed the lights and projected a map his office had compiled showing nuclear dump sites across the U.S.: tiny death's-heads speckled the screen like fly spots on a napkin. He said these sites would be unin-habitable for a million years. There were many death's-heads, and the audience got silent. As Jerry ran through the statistics on radioactive sludge, Susanna fiddled with the headset and listened to him in French and Italian female voices.

When the house lights came back on, the ecologists blinked grumpily and lit up. "Questions?" said Jerry and someone called out, "What action is being taken?" But Jerry could only stammer and hedge like a White House press corps frontman, like someone who'd work for nu-clear dumpers instead of struggling against them. "It's difficult," he said. "Mostly our work so far has been to identify sites, inform local residents, and begin to put pressure on the government. Otherwise, it's hard to know just what action to take . . ." He smiled the same silly smile with which he asked Susanna if he could pin her hands behind her head.

A palpable dissatisfaction rose from the audience, min-gling with the smoke from their French cigarettes. Su-sanna wished Jerry had told the stories he'd told in the college bar, the break-ins at his office, the hard disks mysteriously crashed, the secret reports sent through the mail that somehow never got there. That would convince the ecologists that he was already risking all, that what he did was critical and not just academic. And who were these professors to fault him for not doing more? Didn't they know that what to do was the central question of Jerry's life?

A professor from Madrid got up and said, "I'm sorry. You must forgive us if we find this . . . hesitance . . . hard to believe. Here in Europe we all grew up watching John Wayne, expecting this from America: instant cowboy justice."

Everyone laughed and Jerry said, "That's the difference right there. We all grew up thinking that John Wayne was a right-wing fascist. You know," he went on, "I used to feel hesitant talking politics to Europeans, I thought you'd had so much sad history, what could I possibly know? But now in terms of suffering I think we're pulling way out ahead of you guys."

After that there was a silence. A lunch break was announced.

In the lobby the morning's speakers were being congratulated and invited to repeat their presentations in glamorous-sounding cities. Susanna and Jerry stood all alone in a circle of dread. No one would make eye contact with them, people went out of their way to avoid them, so that when at last someone approached, Jerry and Susanna turned away and had to turn back awkwardly when the person started talking.

The tall young man before them was someone Susanna had noticed; it would have been hard not to, he stood out from the crowd. He was dressed in a leather jacket and jeans, with greasy shoulder-length blond hair and an earring; he looked like a movie villain's psycho right-hand man. Perhaps he was an ecoterrorist—there had to be some of them here—and Susanna braced herself for his righteous attack on Jerry.

Instead, in a heavy accent he said, "I think you are very brave man. We all know your Pentagon and C.I.A. are vicious crazy killers. I am Gabor Szekaly. Greenpeace. From Hungaria. Forgive my English is not good."

"Your English is great," said Susanna. "I mean, compared to our Hungarian."

"You speak Hungarian?" said Gabor.

"No," said Susanna. "I just meant—"

"I don't know about *brave*," Jerry said. "But from time to time it does get hairy. My office gets broken into more often than Zsa Zsa Gabor's hotel room."

"Gabor?" said Gabor.

"An actress," Jerry explained. "With lots of heavily insured diamond jewelry that keeps getting ripped off in Las Vegas."

"Hungarian?" said Gabor.

"Originally," said Susanna. "But no one you'd want to know."

Gabor smiled and lowered his head and kissed Susanna's hand. She noticed that his earring was a tiny Coptic cross, and felt guilty for finding his kiss so pleasurable and disturbing.

"Welcome to the conference," Gabor said. "We will be seeing each other, okay?" He turned on his heel and headed across the lobby, a funny walk with elements of a swagger and a scurry.

"Great," said Jerry. "Terrific. Wouldn't you know

Count Dracula would be the one guy who liked my speech?"

The conference became like the mother ship, feeding and sustaining them. After one day Susanna and Jerry stopped leaving the hotel. The ecologists warmed up to Jerry and flirted with Susanna. There were lots of internal politics which Susanna didn't get but which lent the panels a buzz of tension; you felt you might be missing something if you didn't go.

Susanna was acutely aware of where Gabor sat in the room. Already he seemed to have bonded with many conference members with whom he talked volubly, pounding their shoulders and arms. He'd brought a girl who appeared only at meals and sat with him, alone in a corner, always in total silence. The girl wore jeans and a denim jacket and smoked like a chimney. She was tragic and spectacular-looking with a mop of black curly hair, but she stayed on the edge of things and didn't flash it, like Susanna.

Three days into the conference Gabor's turn came to speak, and he ran up to the microphone like a boxer jogging into the ring. Susanna half expected him to vault the seminar table. Angrily he seized the mike and began shouting in Hungarian, rattling off the difficult sounds at the speed of Spanish. All the translation channels went dead; you could almost hear the translators wondering how to proceed—wondering did they have to shout to convey Gabor's meaning? At last they fell back on their calm, expressionless translatorese.

"We are in a time of terrible crisis," Susanna heard on the English channel, "a time that calls for immediate action." Gabor pounded his fist on the table. "Terrible violence is being done to us and we must retaliate, lash ourselves to the back of the whales and wait for the terrible Japanese whalers; we must tie ourselves to the tracks of the terrible nuclear trains. Or better yet we must disable the trains and sink the terrible ships."

Gabor went on for a long while, yelling and beating the table. Finally he finished and rushed out into the hall. After a round of wild applause the audience followed him out. While the others stopped at the coffee cart, Susanna and Jerry found Gabor, who was sweating profusely and making snuffling noises.

"I loved your speech," said Susanna. "I mean I really loved it. It's so important to remind people that we haven't got time, that we must stop talking and act—" She stopped in mid-sentence because her face felt hot and also because her tone—and for all she knew, her actual words—were horrifyingly familiar. It was what she'd said to Jerry after his speech at her college. She thought, I am the lowest of the low. I am an ecology groupie. She glanced at Jerry to see how he was reacting. He was shaking Gabor's hand. "Good work," Jerry said.

"It is so frustrating," Gabor said. "Who knows is anyone listening. To speak of these things is like giving dancing lessons to fucking corpses. I am sorry, I am when I get vexated all the time saying fucking. Even speaking to audience I say, fucking this, fucking that. How did they translate 'fucking'?"

" 'Terrible,' " said Susanna.

" 'Terrible'?" Gabor laughed. "Oh, these Italians are too much. Always thinking the Pope is watching. You take your meals here at the hotel?"

"We have been," said Jerry, "though the food isn't great . . ."

"We have dinner," said Gabor. "At seven."

After her shower, Susanna put on her little white dress, then thought this was the wrong attire for lashing oneself to a whale, and changed into a black T-shirt and black jeans. "You're wearing that?" said Jerry.

Gabor and the girl were in their usual corner. When he saw them he lifted his glass and toasted them from across the room. The girl was even younger than she'd seemed—a brooding Slavic teen. She stuck out her hand and solemnly pumped theirs, once each, up and down hard.

Gabor said, "This is my wife, Maritsa. She is Yugoslavian. Unfortunately she has no English."

"She speaks Hungarian, no?" said Susanna. When had *she* begun framing sentences as if English weren't her language?

"No," said Gabor, smiling. "And I have no Slovenian."

"But they're similar languages?" said Jerry.

"Totally different," said Gabor. "We have no common speech. But we are only married three weeks."

"Obviously, that explains it," Jerry said. "Not long

enough to have to talk. Anyway, congratulations. And here's an amazing coincidence—*we* were married three weeks ago, too."

"Good! Very good!" said Gabor, and lightly punched Jerry's arm. "The language is no problem—but food! Yugoslavians are the world's worst cooks!" He pulled Maritsa to him: she let herself be pulled. Gabor said, "Before we are married we know each other only one week. It is so sudden—like this!" He grabbed his T-shirt over his heart and bunched it up in his hand.

Susanna looked at Gabor, then at Maritsa, then down at the floor. "Great shoes," she said to Maritsa.

"Yugoslavian worker shoes," said Maritsa. She had a deep voice and an outthrust lower lip that gave her a permanent pout. Her skin was geisha white and on each cheek was a harsh smear of rouge, like a bruise. "You do speak English," Susanna said. Maritsa looked at Gabor.

"Everyone admire her shoes," he explained. "So that much at least she learns to say in every European language. Come now. Sit down. We must order."

Gabor stopped Jerry and Susanna from ordering the zuppa di pesce. "Mussels from Adriatic? Suicide!" he said.

Over their bruschetti and antipasti misti they talked about mutant algae. "We hear mutant," said Gabor, who turned out to be not just an ecoterrorist but also a biology professor at Budapest University. "But who knows? Even science news is manipulated. Until now. Wonderful!

Everyone in Budapest is falling in love and buying electronic equipment! But algae we know is big." He held his hands out wide. "In Venice is big problem. This algae is big like—" He held up the hem of the tablecloth. "You say . . . ?"

"Tablecloth," said Susanna.

"Tablecloth," Maritsa repeated. Susanna and Jerry smiled encouragingly.

"Algae like tablecloth!" said Gabor.

Susanna said, "Where did you learn English?"

"In England," Gabor said. " 'Fifty-six. Someone put me on back of motorcycle. I am ten year old. They take me to England and put me with professor's family. Very *sympathique*. I stay five years, learn English, then the daughter gets pregnant, the professor has me deported back to Hungaria."

"He deported you?" said Susanna.

"An ethics professor," Gabor said. He looked at Maritsa, then back at Susanna and Jerry. "Well, okay, anyway, there is more to life than algae like tablecloths."

"Amen!" said Jerry. Susanna leaned so far forward she pulled sharply back, afraid she might have singed her bangs in the candle. Maritsa touched Susanna's arm in a calming, maternal way.

"Not that you would know from this conference," Gabor said. "Speeches, speeches. I am sick. Like school. Tomorrow I am not going to panels. I am tired. Tomorrow we look at art. I know very well Milan museums. You will come?"

Jerry said, "I think I should stick around. Susanna can go if she wants."

The hotel lobby was glossy black with an atrium skylight admitting one dramatic shaft of light, like a Weimar nightclub crossed with a Mongolian yurt. Maritsa huddled in a corner of the black leather couch, practically hugging the standing ashtray. Gabor lounged beside her with his back to a mirrored column. "Did you sleep well?" he asked.

"Fine," Susanna said.

It felt good to be wearing blue jeans in this lobby full of Armani; crossing it, they fell into a companionable pack-like stride. Gabor hailed a cab and held the door for the women, then jumped in beside the driver and began gabbing in Italian. Maritsa stretched her legs till her feet touched the front seat. Susanna had never felt so stiff-backed and prim, it was a new experience. When Gabor stopped talking, the driver shrugged and hit the gas. Maritsa and Susanna went flying as they squealed around a curve.

Gabor wheeled around in his seat and said excitedly to Susanna, "Ayi, I love how these guys drive! They are the real cowboys. Not that pig John Wayne, your husband was right. Is nothing to ride a horse alone in desert. But to drive a hundred kilometers an hour in traffic! This trip will cost monthly salary of average Hungarian professor. Lucky, Milan is paying—" He broke off for an argument with the driver about directions.

"How do you know the city so well?" asked Susanna.

"On the way back from England I live awhile in Italy. Again, romantic trouble, is best for me to take off. Now that I have my Maritsa I am through with all that stuff." He twisted even further around so he and Maritsa could lock gazes.

Gabor did know the museums; he was a connoisseur of sorts. His taste ran to trompe l'oeil and dark late Renaissance narrative paintings of bizarre miracles. He was a great fan of Archimboldo's—"vegetable pipple," he called them.

"This is my favorite painting," he said, in front of an immense canvas entitled *The Miracle of the Bees*. In the painting a crowd was gathered around a baby from whose mouth issued a swarm of bees, curling up toward the ceiling. At least a dozen times he said, "This is my favorite painting," and hurried from favorite to favorite, ignoring everything else.

Nothing could have been further from Jerry's Michelin approach, and it exhilarated Susanna to be hustled past the tourists with their guidebooks. Gabor was eager to show them an elegant stiletto hidden in a Renaissance crucifix. He said, "This was made to be used only once. God, I love the Italians!"

They took cabs from museum to museum, like barhopping, thought Susanna. They wound up near the Duomo, Gabor yelling at the cabdriver as they hunted for the Ambrosian Library. Finally Gabor jumped out

and grabbed Maritsa's hand and pulled her inside a building and up a long stone staircase. Susanna skipped along
after. "What's the hurry?" she said.

"Hurry is because we are approaching my favorite
painting," Gabor said. "Not my favorite. MY FAVOR-
ITE. Many times I say favorite but this I mean is my
favorite. Astonishing, no?"

It was astonishing, all right—Bramantino's *The Virgin
Enthroned with Saints*—an unexceptional Mother and
Child, the ordinary saints, but on the floor at Mary's feet
were two gigantic figures lying on their backs, drawn in
showy perspective so you looked from behind their heads
to their feet. On the left was a corpse—was it Christ?—
and on the right was a human-sized dead frog. The corpse
was naked but the frog was dressed in knee breeches and
a livery jacket.

Maritsa pointed to the frog and said something in Slovenian. "Frog," said Susanna, and Gabor said the Hungarian word for frog.

"This is your favorite painting?" said Susanna. "Your
favorite favorite?"

Gabor shrugged. "I like this frog. Is funny. It gives me
a feeling. In all Milan is nothing gives me such strong
feeling. Except maybe that Piero, that egg hanging from
a string. But I think not as much as this frog."

Really, the most astonishing thing was how wretched
this made Susanna. So Gabor liked a picture with a
peculiar frog—why should that make her think her whole
life was a misunderstanding and she would have to dis-

assemble it all to begin to straighten it out? She had married the wrong person, ended up in the wrong place. It wasn't as if she'd trade Jerry for a crazy Hungarian whose favorite painting was a Virgin enthroned with Christ and a frog. But Gabor reminded her of what she had forgotten. Somehow she had forgotten that for some people it's fine, it's enough if something's funny and gives you a feeling. She was so tired of everything having to teach you a lesson, preferably a lesson about the end of the world.

"Coffee at once!" said Gabor. "Doctor Gabor's orders! That way, too, is art like food—too much can make you sleepy."

Not far from the Ambrosian they found a bar and went in and stood at the railing. Gabor ordered three espressos and three rakis. "You know raki?" he said. "Is Turkish. Very good for too much museum." He tossed back his raki and chased it with the espresso. Maritsa coolly did the same, and Susanna had no choice.

"Stamp-collector bar," Gabor said. "Sundays, stamp collectors set up tables in the square for buying and trading, and when they finish they come here and drink grappa." In fact, the walls were decorated with murals of giant stamps, and maybe on Sundays it drew a philatelist crowd, but right now it looked like a gay bar. Young men stood in couples and in little groups. Feeling better than she had in the museum, Susanna held up her raki glass. "Works like magic," she told Gabor.

"I tell you!" said Gabor and ordered another round of

raki and another espresso. "Doctor Gabor prescribes!"

Both bartenders were peasant women, straight off the farm or the vineyard, still in housedresses and aprons, unusual in this city where everyone dressed like salespeople in boutiques. They were chatting with a customer, a woman the size of a ten-year-old, dark-skinned, probably gypsy. Two braids hung to her waist. She wore a faded floor-length skirt and a kid's long-sleeved striped polo shirt. A curly-haired child clung to her skirt. Susanna recalled an older child they'd passed playing in the doorway. The woman puffed angrily on her cigarette as she chattered to the barmaids in Italian. She kept pacing and turning sharply with little disdainful shakes of her hip.

"I love the gypsies," Gabor said. "They are tough people, believe me. After we fail, Greenpeace, conferences, all this blah-blah, everything failed, poisoned, civilization bye-bye, the gypsies will still be here when all of us are *finito.*"

"Not cauliflowers?" said Susanna.

"Please?" Gabor said.

"The raki is something," she said. Even Maritsa, she noticed, was starting to look a bit green.

"One more. And espresso," said Gabor. "Then we will have the right dose."

After that round Susanna knew it had been a drastic mistake. The world around her got painfully loud, then syrupy and slow. All at once she was aware of the gypsy woman watching her. She felt as if she were watching herself, and she thought distinctly: "I am having a hallucination."

The vision couldn't have lasted more than a few seconds, but in that time she saw the end of the world, empty canyons of buildings in a depopulated city, like some post-nuclear Hollywood set, except that it was Milan, deserted but for the gypsy woman and her children, sashaying idly in and out of empty restaurants and shops, bored and petulant, neither happy nor sad that all this was now theirs. Susanna watched for a while and then it rushed away, and she felt herself rising over Milan, over Italy, then above the earth, not the familiar earth, pockmarked, green and blue. This was a new earth, a bald earth, shining in the black sky, white and brilliant and polished, like a ping-pong ball lit from within.

The next thing Susanna knew, she was in her hotel bed looking up at Jerry. For a moment she saw his face as an Archimboldo: cauliflower skin, carrot nose, green-bean eyeglass frames. He said, "Raki and espresso. Dynamite combination."

"Gabor?" she said.

"He was abject," said Jerry. "I gather it was quite a scene, him carrying you cave-man style through the lobby." Jerry was smiling at her. His voice was nasal with false urgency, like a forties newsreel announcer.

"I think I'm sick," said Susanna. "I was hallucinating."

Jerry said, "Raki isn't Dr Pepper."

Susanna said, "Jerry, the weirdest thing. I had a vision,

a hallucination. But before that there was a moment
. . . it was like sometimes we'd be in cathedrals with
those machines you plug a hundred lire in to light up
the frescoes for a minute. Always, just before the minute
was up, I'd see something in the paintings. But when the
light went out I would lose it and forget what it was.
Well, there was a gypsy woman in the café, and just
before I felt so strange, I looked at her and thought,
She looks exactly like me. We could be twins and she
knows it. Of course it was ridiculous. We looked nothing
alike."

Jerry stretched out beside her and gazed down into her
face. How old he looks, she thought guiltily, how unhappy and exhausted. Everything showed in his face,
everything they both knew now, that they could not go
on together, their marriage would have to end and she
would have to leave him to face the death of the planet
without her. She knew that Jerry was seeing in her the
heartlessness of the young: unlike him, she still had time
to fix some part of the world, and if it was ending, she
still had the strength to enjoy what was left. And who
was Jerry, really, to make her feel guilty about it?

"You don't look anything like a gypsy," said Jerry. "You
look like Tinker Bell."

Tears came to Susanna's eyes. "I know that," she said,
not because it was true but to fill the silence in which
she might otherwise have to face the fact that she had
married a man to whom she looked like Tinker Bell. An
unpleasant buzzing in her head reminded her of Gabor's

painting. Was the miracle the appearance of the bees or the getting them out of the baby? She said, "It was just a feeling I had that something was telling me something."

"Telling you something?" said Jerry. "Please. Keep your feet on the ground."

RUBBER

LIFE

THAT WINTER I READ a lot and worked in the public library. A fog settled in on my heart like the mists that hung in the cranberry bogs and hid the ocean so totally that the sound of the waves could have been one of those records to help insomniacs fall asleep. Always I'd been happy when the summer people left, but that fall I couldn't look up when the geese flew overhead and I avoided the streets on which people were packing their cars. Always I'd felt that the summer people were missing something, missing the best part of something, but now it seemed that I was the one being left as they went off, not to their winter office life, but to a party to which I had not been asked, and I felt like you do when the phone doesn't ring and no mail comes and it's obvious no one wants you. Of course I had reason to feel that way. But oddly, I hadn't noticed. How strange that you can be satisfied with your life till the slamming of some stranger's car trunk suddenly wakes you up.

I was trying to be civilized, cooking fresh produce till the market ran out, although it was only for me. The house I was caretaking had a microwave oven that seemed important to resist. The microwave surprised me. It was a colonial whaler's house, white clapboard with a widow's walk, so perfectly restored and furnished so obsessively with period pieces that all the comforts of modern life were tucked away grudgingly in some hard-to-find wing or upstairs. There was a cherrywood table on which I read while I ate. I had promised myself: no television till 10:30, when *Love Connection* came on. I loved that show with its rituals of video dating, its singles who rarely loved each other as much as they'd loved each other's images on TV.

The house was supposed to be haunted—but so was every house in our town; a resident ghost could double what you could ask for summer rent. The Carsons, who were returning from Italy in the spring, told me their house had a ghost they'd never seen or heard; they could have been referring to some projected termite problem that never materialized. I didn't listen too hard. I'd heard similar stories in several previous houses, and such was my mood that fall that it depressed me to admit that ghosts were yet another thing that I no longer believed in.

I read through the evenings and weekends. I found out how not to OD. When I got tired there were books I could read for refreshment, fat non-fiction bestsellers detailing how rich people contract-murdered close relatives. I skimmed these books as fast as I could and let their simple sentences wash through my brain like shampoo.

I couldn't read at work, except on quiet mornings. We were surprisingly busy. Our town had a faithful daytime library crowd—young mothers, crazies, artists, retirees, the whole range of the unemployed and unattached. The best part of my job was seeing them come in from the briny winter cold, into the shockingly warm, bright library where the very air seemed golden with the fellowship and grateful presence of other people.

At first I read mostly new books, picked indiscriminately from the cartons that came in. Most of them were boring, but I liked knowing how to live with tennis injuries and diseases I hoped never to live with. I preferred these to books about why women lose men, books that made me so anxious I'd fall asleep reading and wake up long before dawn. It was a winter of lengthy biographies: lives that seemed longer than lives lived in actual time. I read a book about Edith Wharton and Henry James, and then I read Edith Wharton. I felt so close to Lily in *The House of Mirth* that when she took opium and died, an odd electric shiver shot across my scalp. We had six Edith Wharton books. When I finished them, nothing else seemed appealing and for a while I felt lost.

Then I became interested in a man named Lewis and the problem of what to read was solved because now I could read what he read. I put aside the books he returned and later took them home. To start, these were mainly cookbooks with photos in which dusty bits of Mexico or Tuscany peeked disconsolately at you from behind shiny platters of food. The first time I noticed Lewis—one of the summer helpers must have issued his card—he was returning a book he opened to show me a huge plate of black pasta on which some mussels had been fetchingly strewn.

"Isn't it wild?" Lewis said. "Isn't it pornographic?"

"How do they make it black?" I said.

"Squid ink," Lewis said. He looked at me almost challengingly, perhaps because our town was very health-conscious, on strict natural and macrobiotic diets that would probably not include squid ink—though you might ask why not. The previous week, at a potluck Sunday brunch, I got up to help clear the dishes and was scraping grapefruit shells into the compost pail when my hostess said, "Stop!" It wasn't compost, it was the tofu casserole main course. After that, the black pasta looked as magnificent as the walled Tuscan city behind it, and when I said, "Have you ever made this?" there was a catch in my voice, as if we were gazing not at pasta but at a Fra Angelico fresco.

Lewis said, "No, I use the pictures for attitude. Then I make up the recipes myself."

I wondered whom he cooked for, but didn't feel I could ask. It crossed my mind he might be gay—but somehow I thought not. After that, I paid attention: Lewis came in about twice a week, often on Mondays and Thursdays; I always wore jeans and sweaters, but on those days I tried to look nice.

One day a Moroccan cookbook seguéd into a stack of books about Morocco which I checked out for him, longing to say something that wasn't obvious ("Interested in Morocco?") or librarian-like ("Oh, are you planning a trip?"). If he was en route to Marrakech, I didn't want to know. When he returned the Morocco books I guiltily sneaked them home. That night I sat at my table and read what he'd read, turned the pages he'd turned, till a hot desert wind seemed to draft through the house, and I felt safe and dozed off.

He chose topics apparently at random, then read systematically: theater memoirs, histories of the Manhattan Project, Victorian social mores, the Dada avant-garde, Conrad, Apollinaire, Colette, Stephen Jay Gould. I read right behind him, with a sense of deep, almost physical connection, doomed and perverse, perverse because to read the same words he'd read felt like sneaking into his room while he slept, doomed because it was secret. How could I tell him that, with so many books in the library, I, too, just happened to pick up *The Panda's Thumb*?

No matter what else Lewis borrowed, there were always a couple of art books. He renewed a huge book on the Sistine Chapel three times and when I finally got it home I touched the angels' faces and ran one finger down the defeated curve of the prophet's shoulders. He often had paint on his clothes, and when I'd convinced myself that it wasn't too obvious or librarian-like, I asked if he was an artist. He hesitated, then went to the magazine shelf and opened a three-month-old *ArtNews* to a review of his New York show. There was a photo of a room decorated like a shrine with tinfoil and bric-a-brac and portraits of the dead in pillowy plastic frames. He let me hold it a minute, then took it and put it back on the shelf. I was charmed that he'd given me it and then gotten shy; other guys would have gone on to their entire résumés. I wanted to say that I understood now how his work was like his reading, but I was ashamed to have been paying attention to what he read. After he left, I got the *ArtNews* and reread it again and again.

Then two weeks passed and Lewis didn't appear. One

afternoon a woman brought back Lewis's books. I noticed the proprietary intimacy with which she handled them; they might have been dishes, or his laundry, unquestionably her domain. She had red hair and a pretty, Irish face, endearingly like mine. She looked around, intimidated. Were it anyone else, I would have asked if she needed help, but I have to confess that I liked it when she left without any books.

The next time Lewis came in, he stood several feet from my desk. "Stand back," he said. "I've still got the flu."

I said, "Look, look at this," babbling mostly to cover the fact that my face had lit up when I saw him. As it happened, we'd just received a new book—a history of the 1918 influenza epidemic. He took it and returned from the shelves with an armload of medical history. In one volume of sepia photos, hollow-eyed Civil War soldiers stared into the camera; for all their bandages and obvious wounds, they perched on the edge of their cots, as if, the instant the shutter snapped, they might jump up and go somewhere else. Lewis said, "I think I'll go home and get over this flu and meditate on a new piece."

Nothing is so seductive as thinking you're someone's muse—even when you aren't—and in that instant the library became for me a treasure trove of possibilities for conversation with Lewis. The cellophane bookcovers seemed to wink with light, and as I browsed among them, I felt like a fish in clear silver water, swimming from lure to lure. Each week I set something aside and rehearsed what I wanted to show him, but always I was defeated by an adrenaline rush.

One day he was practically out the door when I called him back and flung open a coffee-table book. I turned to a photo of an altar from a West African tribe that boasted an elaborate dream culture in which you constructed little personal shrines with doll figures representing everyone you had ever slept with in a dream.

Lewis studied it awhile. Then he said, "My gallery isn't big enough." I laughed but it hurt me a little. I thought, Well, it serves me right. Honestly, I couldn't believe what I'd picked out to finally show him.

Lewis said, "And who do *you* dream about?" It was a smarmy, lounge-lizard kind of question he seemed shocked to hear himself ask. Then he got embarrassed and I got embarrassed and I said, "Last night I dreamed I was trapped in Iran with terrorists looking for me and—"

"Oh," said Lewis, semi-glazed over. "The evening-news dream. Do you get cable? The worst dreams I ever have are from falling asleep watching C-Span government hearings from D.C."

A week or so later I ran into Lewis on Front Street. I had never seen him out in the world. It took me a second to recognize him; then my heart started slamming around. I walked toward him, thinking I would soon get calm, but when I reached him I was quite breathless and could barely speak. He walked me to the library. I noticed that we moved slower and slower, the closer and closer we got; it made me feel I should be looking around for the woman Lewis lived with. He said he was driving to Rockport next week and did I want to go? He left me at the library without coming in, even though it was Thursday, one of his regular days.

On the way to Rockport, Lewis told me his idea. He was planning to make a kind of wax-museum diorama, all manner of Civil War wounded and maimed behind a plexiglass panel that tinted everything sepia except in large gaps through which you could see the scene in all its full gory color. When I asked what he needed in Rockport he said, "I don't know. Store mannequins. Ace bandages. Ketchup. Half my art is shopping."

I tried to imagine the piece, but kept being distracted by how many layers of meaning everything seemed to have. For example: the ashtray in his car was full and smelled awful. Normally, I'd have shut it, but he wasn't smoking, so it must be the woman he lived with who smoked, and I feared my shutting the ashtray might be construed and even intended as a movement toward him, against her. I felt she was there with us in the car; in fact, it was her car. I can't remember quite what I said but I know that it wasn't entirely connected to Lewis's saying, "It's Joanne's car. Joanne, the woman I live with."

"How long have you lived together?" I asked; my voice sounded painfully chirpy.

"Forever," said Lewis, staring off into space. "Forever and ever and ever."

Rubber Life

By then we were walking through Rockport at our usual hypnotized crawl; really, it was so cold you'd think we might have hurried. Lewis bought a wall clock, the plain black-and-white schoolroom kind. In a dry-goods shop, he asked to see the cheapest white bedsheets they had, and the salesman looked at me strangely. We walked in and out of antique stores; several times Lewis made notes. More often, we just window-shopped. In front of one crowded window, Lewis pointed to a large porcelain doll in a rocking chair. He said, "People always say 'lifelike' when they just mean nicely painted. But that one really looks like an actual dead child."

"Or a *live* one," I said, overbrightly. Though the doll was fairly extreme, I probably wouldn't have noticed. Whatever I was drawn to in antique shop windows, it wasn't, hadn't been for years, the Victorian doll in the rocker with the corkscrew curls and christening dress. But when Lewis said look, I looked.

It would have seemed impolite not to ask him in for a drink when he drove me home, and when it got late and I said, "Won't Joanne be expecting you?" and he said, "She's in Boston," it would have seemed silly not to invite him to dinner. Hadn't my asking after Joanne made my good intentions clear? If you believed *that*, you'd believe that my showing him the African dream-lover altar was meant to convey not the fact that I'd dreamed of sleeping with him (which, actually, I hadn't) or that I wanted to sleep with him, but rather that I would be satisfied if it only happened in dreams.

There was never any telling when he would show up. Sometimes at night he would rap on the window, very *Wuthering Heights*, and my heart would jump. I'd think first of psycho killers and then of the house's ghost; then I'd realize it was Lewis and get scared in a different way. We were very discreet because of Joanne. He clearly felt torn for deceiving her and would never come, or say he would come, unless she was gone or too busy to ever suspect or find out.

In the library we were distant, no different from before. It was remarkably erotic. Once more I brought home the books he returned, read what he had read, though now these were sometimes on woodworking and the chemistry of glue. Strangely, I never mentioned this. I think I was superstitious that his knowing might spoil my pleasure, pleasure I badly needed to fill the time between his visits. I was disturbed that time had become something to fill, and sometimes I couldn't help wondering if I hadn't been happier before.

But of course I never wondered that when Lewis was around. I made him watch *Love Connection* with me, and for the first time my feelings for the video-date couples were unmixed with personal fear. He seemed so happy to see me that I thought, without daring to think it in words, that what he felt was love. But how could I know the truth about this when I never knew him well enough to confess we read the same books? There were some things I knew. He used to bring me presents: sewing baskets, beaded purses, bits of antique fluffery that some-how I knew he'd tried out unsuccessfully in his work. Lewis often talked of his work in the most astonishing ways. Once he told me about making a figure for his new piece, a Confederate dummy. Just as he finished painting the face, he was for an instant positive he'd seen it blink, and he felt that if he sat down beside it on its cot he might stay there and never get up.

One night he gave me a cardboard box long enough for a dozen roses, but wider. In it was the Victorian doll we'd seen in the Rockport window. Though it wasn't something I wanted, I nonetheless burst into tears and, like an idiot, I hugged it. I stood there lamely, cradling the doll, wondering where to put it. I thought of pet-shop goldfish and of how one was cautioned to find them a water temperature just like the one they had left, and I remembered the antique mini-rocking chair in the Car-sons' living room, with the tiny woven counterpane tossed artfully across it, always at the ready to keep the colonial baby warm. The doll was larger than it appeared, and it was a bit of a squeeze. For a while we remained looking down at it until it had stopped rocking.

That night when we were in bed we heard footsteps from downstairs. "Did you hear that?" I said, though I could tell Lewis had. It had stopped us cold. Lewis put on his pants and picked up a poker from the fireplace in my bedroom, a hearth I suddenly wondered why I had never used. "Wait here," he said, but I put on my night-gown and followed him.

We skulked through the house, flinging doors open, like in the movies. But there was no one there. The door was locked, the windows shut. Nothing had been disturbed. "Mice," Lewis said.

"Mice in tap shoes," I said.

Then Lewis said, "Look at that." The doll we'd left in the rocker was sitting in one corner of the living room couch. He said, "How did you do *that*?"

"I didn't!" I said shrilly. "I was upstairs with you." I felt too defensive to be frightened or even amazed. Did he think I'd staged this for his benefit? I'd read all those books for his benefit, and I couldn't even admit that. "Well, the house is supposed to be haunted," I said, and then got terribly sad. It struck me that finding yourself in a haunted house with someone should unite you in a kind of fellowship, the camaraderie of the besieged, of spookiness and fear. But I didn't sense any of that. What I did feel was that Lewis had moved several steps away. "Put it back in the rocker," he said.

"I don't think it liked it there," I said.

"Put the doll back in the rocker," he said. I did, and we went upstairs. We got into bed and curled back to back, staring at opposite walls. Finally he said, "I'm sorry. I take these things too seriously. I guess it was being raised Catholic. I can't help thinking it has something to do with Joanne."

I couldn't see what a walking doll could have to do with Joanne. I hadn't known he was Catholic—why had that never come up? I didn't know why this was stranger than thinking a Confederate dummy had blinked at him.

"I'm Catholic, too," I said. "But the ghost is a Protestant ghost."

Just then the footsteps resumed. We rolled over and looked at each other. It was exactly like those awful moments when you wake up in the morning and the pain you've been worried about is still there.

Downstairs, we found the doll on the couch. This time I got frightened. Lewis's face looked totally different than I'd ever seen it.

"You know what, Bridget?" he said to me. "You are one crazy chick."

After that, everything changed and ground to a gradual halt. After that, the doll stayed put and we never discussed that night. To mention it would have risked letting him know how wronged I felt, not just over his coolness, his punishing me for what obviously wasn't my fault, but because he'd left me so alone, alone with my own astonishment. I'd been mystified, too, confused, even a little irritated to find myself so chilled by something I couldn't explain and didn't believe in. I kept thinking that meeting a ghost with someone who actually loved you might actually have been fun. Anyway, what was happening with us seemed beyond discussion. In the library, we acted the same as before, but it was no longer exciting. It left me nervous and sad. I stopped reading the books he brought back. All I had to do was look at them and a heaviness overcame me, that same pressure in the chest that on certain days warns you it's not the right time to start leafing through family albums of the family dead.

I no longer read at all. Without that awareness of what Lewis might choose, I'd lost my whole principle of selection. Out of habit, I browsed the shelves; nothing seemed any less boring than anything else. I gave up *Love Connection*, but often fell asleep watching TV, not for entertainment so much as for steadiness, comfort, and noise. For a while I forgot the doll, then considered throwing it out. I wound up tossing the counterpane over its head and leaving it in its chair; the doll showed no reaction. I remember waves of a tingly frostbite chill, a physical burning that sent me racing to the mirror. Naturally, nothing showed. It should not have been so painful, the whole thing had been so short-lived, not nearly so bad as, say, the breakup of a long marriage, losing someone you've shared years and children with. That pain is about everything: your life, your childhood, death, your past. Mine was purely about the future.

That winter the future took a very long time to come. I felt that time had become an abyss I would never get across. And then at last it was spring. The Carsons returned from Italy. Their eyes kept flickering past me till they'd reassured themselves that the house was in perfect shape. Then they thanked me for forwarding their mail, inquired after my winter, told me that Florence had been marvelous fun, and asked if I'd seen the ghost. No, I said. I hadn't.

"No one has," said Mrs. Carson. "But once you know about it . . . Now that you're leaving, I can tell you. I'm always reluctant to lease this place to couples with small children because the ghost, oh, it's horrible, the ghost is supposed to be that of a child."

For just a moment I got the chills. I refused to let this sink in. I wondered if her reluctance really had to do with the supernatural or with damage control. I said, "Well, if that's the case, I'm leaving the ghost a present." I indicated the doll. They weren't exactly thrilled. The doll, after all, was Victorian, hopelessly out-of-period. They seemed already tired of me and impatient for a reunion with their possessions.

Outside, packed, was the car I had just bought; even its monthly-payment book seemed a sign of faith in the future. I was moving to Boston to enroll in a library science program. I said goodbye to the Carsons and got in my car and drove off. On my way out of town, I drove past the golf course on which, from the corner of my eye, I spotted what looked like a sprinkling of brilliant orange poppies. It took me a while to realize that they were plastic tees.

Moments of recovery are often harder to pinpoint than moments of shock and loss, but I knew then at what precise instant I'd stopped grieving over Lewis. It had been late April, or early May, a few weeks before the Carsons came home. The tulips were in bloom. I'd been at work, shelving books, deep in the stacks. A volume on Coptic religious texts had fallen open to reveal a magazine hidden inside. It was a fetish magazine called *The Best of Rubber Life*. Inside were color photos of mostly plump, mostly female couples. Some of the women wore baby-doll pajamas, others were in rubber suits or in the process of putting them on. Most were in quasi-sexual poses though no one seemed to be touching or making love. Everyone gazed at the camera, full frontal stares in some hard-to-read middle between totally blank and bold.

I wondered whose it was. I considered some (mostly elderly) men who seemed like possible candidates. I thought meanly: maybe it was Lewis's. But I didn't think so. Perhaps I should have been disgusted, it was really extremely sordid, or even frightened of being in the library with whoever had hid it there. In fact, I felt nothing like that, but rather a funny giddiness, an unaccountable lightness of heart. I felt remarkably cheered up. Standing there in the stacks, turning the pages, I realized, as never before, what an isolated moment each photograph represents, one flash of light, one frozen instant stolen from time, after which time resumes. It was what I'd thought when I'd first seen those Civil War pictures but had never known how to tell Lewis. Perhaps I'd been worried that if I told him, the camera would click and he'd move.

I looked at the women in the rubber magazine, and I began to laugh, because all I could think of was how soon the strobes would stop flashing, the cameras would click one last time, how that day's session would end, and they would collect their checks and rise from their rubber sheets and fill the air with hilarious sounds as they stripped off their rubber suits. It was almost as if I could hear it, that joyous sigh and snap—the smacky kiss of flesh against flesh, of flesh, unbound, against air.

AMAZING

IN THE UPSTAIRS BEDROOM, three teenage girls lay on top of a pile of coats, watching Yasir Arafat with the sound turned off. "Neat headscarf," said one. "Too bad he looks like Ringo Starr."

How sweet it would have been to fall back on the bed and stare up at the high white ceiling and listen forever to the liquid murmuring voices of these girls! But Grady couldn't do that, he was working, he was supposed to be giving a puppet show at the children's party downstairs. Also he was anxious about Harry, his six-year-old son, who'd come to the party with him and been sent down to the basement where the other children were.

Three parties were going at once, one on top of the other. The TV teens were upstairs, the children on the bottom, and, sandwiched in the middle, adults. It had taken forever to find this place, out in the woods near Katonah. Grady kept missing the unmarked driveway, which, when he found it, went on so long he gave up in the middle and turned and drove back to the road. Harry had fallen silent. "We are not lost," Grady told him. "We are absolutely not lost." At last they reached a clearing and a perfect Victorian house so grand Grady felt he should be seeing it from above, in an aerial shot under the titles of some prime-time weekly soap opera.

On his way downstairs he drifted past other bedrooms; everywhere, platform beds and pedestal TVs seemed to levitate slightly off the dove-gray industrial carpeting. The hall was High Victorian, the bedrooms High Tech, so that crossing a doorsill often meant a hundred-year jump in time. Grady bypassed the grownup party and continued down to the basement—a huge room, dramatically lit through a band of high windows beneath the ceiling. The polished wood floor was covered with Turkish kilims on which a dozen children were greedily helping themselves to the pleasures of Space Age child heaven: video games, a robot, a wall-sized TV showing vintage Betty Boop. The noise was unspeakable—volleys of shooting rockets and maddening video tunes. Grady lingered long enough to see that Harry had found an inflated brontosaurus and was gently punching it back and forth with another little boy. Then he went upstairs.

The bar was set out on a carved oak hutch. Grady hovered nearby with a hopeful expression that eventually drew his hostess—a pretty, blond woman with sparkly girlish eyes that seemed startled to find themselves looking at you from so many spidery lines. A slight tic kept pulling one eye to the side, as if she wanted to wink at you but kept changing her mind.

"I'm Caroline," she said. "Did I say that before? Can I fix you a drink? Would that be all right? What would Miss Manners say?" Grady knew what she meant. Even when they themselves were feverishly drinking away the longueurs of a children's party, the parents who hired him almost never offered him drinks. It was as if he were one of the children, or had been hired to drive them somewhere instead of just entertain them.

Grady smiled. "Miss Manners would say bourbon, a little ice. Please. Thank you." Caroline laughed and poured him a big glass of bourbon.

"You really shouldn't," she said. "Bourbon has the most toxins." Even as it occurred to Grady that this was her way of flirting, some note in her voice made him realize which of the TV-watching girls was hers. He was thinking of how to say this when he looked past the hutch and saw a photo of Mr. Rogers grinning at him from the wall.

"Gee," Grady said. "I'm finding it a little hard to drink this with Mr. Rogers watching."

"Oh," said Caroline. "I don't think Fred would object." She spoke warningly, as people do when you are about to slander someone and they signal you: *Careful. This is a friend*.

"Do you mind if I ask," Grady said, "why you have a framed photo of Mr. Rogers on your wall?"

"I don't know if you know," said Caroline, "but we have two sets of kids." She gestured up at the ceiling and down at the floor. "The girls are from previous marriages, but Walt is our joint production. I used to watch Mr. Rogers with my first family, then I started watching him again with Walt. And there Fred Rogers was, still hanging in there. I wrote him a fan letter, and he sent me a very nice note."

"That's wonderful," Grady mumbled. Barbara used to say that Mr. Rogers was the last guy in the world she would leave Harry alone in a room with. But he couldn't tell Caroline that. It was a year since Barbara left—a year and two months, exactly. A year before that, a car had rear-ended her at a stop sign and left her in constant intractable pain from a headache nothing could touch.

They'd seen a dozen doctors and at some point half the doctors asked: *What happened to the car?* It was embarrassing to have to say: *Only one taillight got smashed.*

Last Christmas Eve, Barbara sent Grady and Harry out for whipping cream for the eggnog. She'd been so specific—they'd driven around for ages till they found the only cream in the county that wasn't ultra-pasteurized—and by the time they got back she had packed and left. Christmas Eve: they would always know precisely how long she'd been gone. Now she called Harry weekly and sent postcards from Berkeley, where she was in herbal therapy with a homeopath from Bombay; her handwriting was unrecognizable, sloppy and round as a child's. In nearly every card, she advised Grady to put sunscreen on Harry, as if she had forgotten they lived in a place with seasons. The longer Grady thought about this, the harder it became to let Caroline know that his silence was not a judgment on her warm feelings for Fred Rogers. Finally Caroline said, "Let's go find my husband. Do you need any help setting up?"

Actually Grady didn't; he'd designed the show that way. Still, he followed Caroline, who was, he sensed, bringing him not for help but to be checked out. She led him through a cathedral-like addition, its rough beams and glass walls suggesting an Alpine ski lodge with guests who had nothing to do but wait for the clouds to part for their personal glimpse of the Matterhorn. The afternoon light made everything look glittery and expensive—the snowy field outside, the tinsel, the candles floating in glass bowls, the gleaming metallic thread shot through the women's sweaters.

The man whose forearm Caroline touched was talking to a pale girl with greased, lacquer-black short hair and wine-red raccoony eye shadow. She smiled once and vanished when Caroline said, "Eliot, this is Grady. Grady's doing Walter's puppets." The man who shook Grady's hand had the serious good looks of certain anchormen who Grady was always shocked to learn were around his own age.

"Eli," he said, with an odd overemphasis that made it hard to tell if he was being friendly or just contradicting his wife. "Good to meet you. Can I get you another drink?" Eli's eyes had a swimmy, unfocused gaze that couldn't quite locate Grady's.

"Puppets," said Eli, refilling Grady's bourbon. "That's amazing." Often guys like Eli said that what Grady did was amazing, mostly in the one-quarter admiring, three-quarters patronizing way people told Barbara: *It's amazing women survive staying home with the kids.* How many of the doctors he'd gone to with Barbara had paused, pen poised above the prescription blank, to tell him how much they wished *they* had talent in the arts.

Grady said, "I've been doing it for five years." He took a big gulp of bourbon. They were leaning against the hutch.

"I know what you mean," Eli said. "Nothing stays amazing for very long. Then *other* things become amazing. You know what amazes me? I don't know half of these people's names." They both stared into the room. Eli said, "This is embarrassing. Forget you heard this. I sound like the middle-aged yuppie Great Gatsby." Suddenly it struck Grady that Eli was really stewed.

Grady put down his glass. He liked having his wits about him. Barbara's leaving had left him feeling a need for extra vigilance about Harry. He kept telling himself that, despite everything, Harry would be all right; that morning Harry had woken him in great excitement to see on TV what looked like the Balinese equivalent of the Rose Bowl parade.

"I've got my puppet stuff in the hall," Grady said. His stage was a rectangular frame, surrounded by curtains he hung at waist level from shoulder straps and put his hands up from underneath. His puppets fit in one large suitcase.

"Is that it?" said Eli. "Amazing." As Grady followed Eli down the basement stairs, a stocky child flew into them with such force that Eli stumbled. "Walt, this is Grady," Eli said. "Grady, my son, Walt. Grady's the puppet man."

The boy was dark-haired and glossily pretty, but with a peculiar, passive-aggressive slump you rarely saw in a child. "Are we having a piñata?" he said.

"No," Grady said. "No piñatas."

"Good," said Eli, "I can't stand piñatas. I've never seen it go down where some kid didn't nearly get brained."

"I want a piñata," Walt said.

"Excuse me," Eli said. "I need to check on something upstairs." Stunned, Grady and the birthday boy watched him leave. The child recovered first, lost interest, and drifted off. Grady hoped Eli would come back. He could, if he had to, do his show marooned with kids on a desert island. But everything went a lot smoother with at least minimal grownup support.

An elderly woman in jeans walked briskly toward him. She had a quick, slightly batty smile and a furrowed, appealing face. "I'm Estelle," she said. "Walt's grandma." Grady could have guessed. Estelle's right eye had the same funny squint as her daughter's.

Estelle said, "I'm Eliot's mom." It touched Grady to think of Eli holding out, through at least one previous marriage, for that tic he must have seen from his cradle and imprinted on like a duck. "You think these little monsters can sit still?" Estelle asked. "I guess you can try, but I doubt it. If it isn't remote control or computer, forget it. If they can't punch a button and tell it what to do, they're not interested."

Not Harry, Grady thought. Harry didn't want to run the world but to be its unnoticed servant. He really had been worried that the driveway to this house would go on forever and never lead them here. Over in the corner, Harry and the kid he'd been dinosaur-punching with were playing with silver blocks, each covered with a foil-like skin of hologram bricks.

Grady rarely started without lots of consultation. When did the parents want him? Before or after the cake? He considered asking Estelle, then decided to take Eli's departure as a sign of total permission. He unpacked the puppets from their case and hung the stage from his shoulders. "All right, kids," he said, "I'd like to introduce you to some puppet friends who've come with me especially for Walt's birthday."

The children hit their respective "off" buttons and trudged toward Grady's stage. When Grady caught Estelle's eye, she drew herself up and saluted. "Flaps up!" Estelle said.

Some days Grady could almost convince himself that Snow White was the greatest story ever told. To meet his seven dwarfs told you all you needed to know about the varieties of human personality. The wicked queen scared even him, and when she made the audience her mirror and asked who was the fairest of them all, the children's voices actually shook as they shouted out, "Snow White!" Today was hardly one of those days—but somehow Grady got through. He even got a little rise out of them when the dwarfs tried to figure out what kind of creature the sleeping Snow White was. "A moose," the children cried. "A rhinoceros." When the queen offered Snow White the poisoned apple, an older kid yelled, "Just say no." Another kid, at another party, had said this a few weeks before.

The children clapped when Snow White and the prince took their bows. Within seconds the place sounded again like a video arcade. Harry and his friend returned to their Mylar blocks, and Estelle came over to watch Grady pack up the puppets. "I adored it," she said. "Of course it's wasted on them."

Amazing

Grady stood beside Estelle, watching the children play. It felt exactly like standing with Eli, observing the grownup party. What completed the circle was a small girl watching a mini-TV on which, Grady realized, was a closed-circuit broadcast from the adult party upstairs. "I worry about this generation," Estelle said. "I mean it. They're growing up so they can't tell computers from people, except that they're nicer to computers. I read in an article that the way things are going, in twenty years people will kill you for two dollars in your pocket. Two dollars!"

"That's inflation," said Grady. "Today it's fifty cents."

He couldn't tell if Estelle's laugh was phony or sincere. After a pause she said, "Take my grandson. Last Christmas I got him a goldfish. The kind you win at the fair and, the next day, down the toilet. The day after Christmas I'm babysitting, I go answer the phone, and when I get back, Walt's got his fist in the bowl, grabbing at the poor fishie like Sylvester the cat. He had the most awful grin on his face, like he knew what he was doing."

"The bad seed," said Grady lightheartedly, so she'd know he didn't mean it even if he did. Officially, he was finished work, but he didn't want to go home. He considered going upstairs, but was hesitant to leave Harry down here with Walt the goldfish-grabber. Finally he excused himself and went up past the living room—he didn't feel strong enough yet to brave that sea of adults —straight to the second floor.

The girls were burrowed deeper in the coat pile, still

watching TV. From the doorway, Grady watched Mother Teresa insisting they rip out the carpet from a mission house she'd been given. "She should have kept the wall-to-wall," said one of the girls. "It would have been more humiliating."

"Closer to the poor," said another girl.

The third girl said, "Last night on *PM Magazine* there was this guy who'd been kidnapped by aliens who told him they had a plan for permanently ending world hunger."

"That's dumb," said the first girl. "You watch *PM Magazine?*"

As soon as Grady went back downstairs, Caroline approached him and said, "We should probably get started."

"Started?" said Grady.

"The puppet show," she said.

"Ended," Grady said. "It only takes half an hour."

"Where was *I*?" Caroline looked so crushed with disappointment that for a second Grady almost offered to repeat the whole show. The moment passed quickly, replaced by the thought that if it had been Mr. Rogers downstairs, she would have been down there watching.

"I'm sorry," she said. "I really am. It's all too much at once. My first husband was a painter and in my first marriage we were always having parties. Afterwards we always fought."

"Parties are work," Grady said.

"It wasn't that," she said. "It was that we felt like each party was a window through which the guests could see our lives, and afterwards we would wonder what they saw, and try to see what they saw, until we would wind up not liking what *we* saw."

Grady's face felt stiff; he was dimly aware of a smile sitting stupidly on his mouth. He didn't know what to say. What if his life was dead-ending here, leaving him stuck forever, unable to either continue this conversation or move? Just then Grady felt a tug on his pants. My little savior! he thought. "How did you find me?" he said, and sank straight to his knees. It was crowded and the people standing nearest him gave him peculiar looks until they saw that he was consoling a child. Then, of course, they smiled. Harry was sobbing so hard he was choking. "Calm down," Grady whispered. "What happened?"

It took Harry a while to talk. "Walt hit me," he said.

"Where?" Grady said. "Hit you where?"

Harry solemnly lifted his shirt. Diagonally across his right shoulder was an ugly welt. "How did he do *that*?" Grady said.

"A sword," Harry said.

"A *sword*?" repeated Grady, this time for Caroline's benefit.

"Oh, God," she said. "His plastic He-Man sword. He's been whacking the shit out of everything with it, and Eliot lets him get away with it."

"What seems to be the problem?" asked Eli.

Grady stood up. "The kids were fighting," he said. He longed to tell Eli to fuck off and grab Harry and get the hell out. But Grady felt he owed it to Harry not to make too much of this—to make him seem like a regular guy who could handle some rough-and-tumble.

"Walt hit me with a sword," Harry said.

"That little monster," Eli said. "Well, he's younger than you. You think you can forgive Walt if he says he's sorry?" Harry nodded tearfully. "All right," said Eli. "Let's go talk to him."

"I don't know," Grady said. "We should really be leaving."

"Not before the *cake*," Eli said to Harry. "Not before the ice cream and *cake*." Harry seemed to agree.

"O.K., we'll stay for some cake," Grady said, and the three of them trooped downstairs. The racket of the video games rose up to meet them. Grady felt suddenly tired; he couldn't remember how many times he'd been led up and down these steps. He thought: I went to a children's party and wound up in Dante's hell.

Walt was jabbing his sword at two little girls he had screaming in a corner. Eli gently disarmed him in a scene with echoes of every hostage movie Grady had ever watched. "Where's Grandma?" Grady asked Eli.

"Oh, Estelle?" said Eliot. "Kids, where's Estelle?" "Oh, I don't know," he told Grady. "The kids probably killed and ate her. One thing about Mom: Dad was a fighter pilot, and now whenever the going gets rough, Mom just parachutes out."

Eli loomed over Walt. He said, "Did you hit this kid?" Only after Walt nodded did Eli kneel. "Say you're sorry," he said.

"I'm sorry," Walt said. Grady knelt, too, and the four of them huddled like some sort of midget scrimmage. "All right!" shouted Eli. "Cake time!"

In a small kitchen adjoining the playroom, refreshments were set out on a rolling cart. On the top tier was the cake, actually a cake system, a series of rectangles iced like a choo-choo train. On the lower tiers were paper plates and forks. Eli wheeled the whole thing in. "Goddamn it," he said. "I should have lit the candles before I made my grand entrance."

Where was Caroline? wondered Grady. If she'd been upset about missing his show, what about missing this? And what about the teen half-sisters up on the second floor? Didn't they want to be here?

"Matches?" Eli said. Grady patted his pockets, though it was years since he'd smoked.

"Wait. I've got the perfect item." Eli took a pistol down from the wall. He aimed at the cake and pulled the trigger.

"I haven't seen one of those in years," Grady said.

Eli smiled. "Not since your fifties finished basement, right? Well, this is my finished basement." He lit the birthday candles with the lighter-gun. "And one for good luck. Can you sing?"

After two dispirited verses of "Happy Birthday," Walt took four tries to blow out the candles. "Gross," said one of the older kids. "You're spitting on the cake."

The cake and ice cream were served buffet style; each child was given a plate. Harry put his plate on the floor by his Mylar blocks. One girl set hers in the outstretched arms of the remote-control robot. "Bad day for the rugs," Grady said.

"Those kilims are tough," Eli said. "Camels have been pissing on them for two thousand years. Come on. I want to show you something."

If Grady had known that Eli meant to lead him upstairs again, he wouldn't have gone. But once they'd set off it was hard to balk and risk revealing that Grady was scared to leave his son with Eli's bad-seed child. Grady took a quick look-round for Harry, and, silently promising to be right back, followed Eli up two flights of stairs.

Eli paused at the door of the room where the girls were watching TV. "My daughter," he said. "Can you believe it?" But he didn't say which daughter was his, and none of the girls turned around. On the screen, a bearded scientist was displaying some red tomatoes he'd cloned from a single cell. "That guy is such a squid," one girl said.

Down the hall, Eli stopped and unlocked a door. It seemed odd, a locked room in your own house, and Grady instantly imagined some Bluebeard scenario, eight former wives stacked against the wall. Instead, they entered a white Victorian room, one wall given over to about twenty built-in TVs. "Fabulous," said Grady. "The man who fell to earth."

"You got it," said Eli, and flicked a switch. Twenty tomatoes, one per screen, came up like a slot machine. "Magic," said Eli. "Clones upon clones." The tomatoes blinked off and twenty images of the scientist-squid took their place. Eli flipped another switch and every screen was different. He waited for Grady to say something. Finally Eli said, "Hey, well, it's tax-deductible." He picked up a glossy magazine and handed it to Grady. On the cover was a photo of Howdy Doody and Buffalo Bob, shot in black-and-white with a dirty, Helmut Newton edge. The name of the magazine was *Television World*. "The family cottage industry," Eli said.

"That's your magazine?" Grady said.

"The first twelve issues paid for this house," Eli said. "It was your textbook business cliché. Find a need and fill it. Plug that hole in the wall of commerce and the dollars pile up. What struck me was that people our age grew *up* on TV, we learned about girls on TV, we learned how to dance, we fought a whole war watching the six o'clock news. So I thought: Why not get some really good writers to write about TV? John Waters on the soaps. Julian Schnabel on Jon Nagy. Turn Hunter Thompson loose on *Miami Vice*. There's an audience, believe me. We have a question-and-answer page, you wouldn't believe the metaphysical stuff that comes in. I'm the publisher, but I also get to write. Right now I'm doing a think piece on what the Brady Bunch did about sex. Don't laugh. You can't imagine Mom and Dad discussing birth control, but from the looks of it, he can only have boys and she can only have girls, so if they had another one . . . Well. We have a column called 'Idea Watch,' someone watches TV all month and counts repeated ideas. Guess how many times in November someone said that men will do anything not to have feelings. You don't watch TV to feel. You watch TV not to feel. Except me." He switched off the twenty sets. "I watch TV to feel."

Eli went over to the window. "Well, not always," he said. "I've had some bad times, too. It's like any other drug. Last week Walt came home from preschool and said it was raining, and I turned on the Weather Channel to see if it was true.

"I'll tell you something," Eli continued. "My family had the first TV on our block. I watched it from my cradle. After school, on weekends, day after childhood day. Now I have what may be the world's largest collection of vintage TV footage. It's a kind of search for me, like some Indian vision quest. Whenever I get time, I watch *Howdy Doody*; *The Honeymooners*; *Have Gun, Will Travel*. If I watch all the shows I watched as a child, maybe I will figure out who that child watching them was. Who *I* was. You know? I thought I would figure out from my son, that I would eventually see in Walt what I used to be. But I can't. My kid is nothing like me."

"They never are," Grady said. But how would he know if Harry was like him? Harry's luck had been so much worse.

"Look," Eli said, and when Grady went to the window, he saw the three teenage girls, bundled in heavy jackets, playing catch in the snow with what appeared to be a phosphorescent tennis ball. Evening was settling in. Where was Harry? Grady felt a shiver of panic. Outside, everything was a grainy bluish-gray, except for the glowing ball and the green sphere of light it cast on the snow as it passed.

"A simple idea," Eli said. "But brilliant. A plastic translucent ball with a hole in it. You break one on those Kaloom sticks, light sticks, and slide it in. I bought two dozen." After some time Eli said, "Are you married?"

"Absolutely," Grady said. He knocked three times on the wooden window ledge, and he and Eli laughed. "I know what you mean," Eli said. "Everything's a tightrope, everything's up in the air. We might stay here. We might still relocate."

"And give up all this?" Grady said.

"Give up all what?" Eli said. "The snow? The cold? We might move to California. *I* might move to California . . ."

The word "California" startled Grady. He had offered to move there with Harry, but Barbara said what she needed now was to concentrate all her energies on getting well. When Grady tried to imagine California, where he had never been, he saw an opaque blue rectangle, a shiny, swimming-pool blue. What else awaited him there? Barbara with her childish handwriting, her crackpot healing theories, that gyroscope point of pain in her head around which her whole life whirled.

"There's a woman there," Eli said. "Naturally she's in television. In L.A." He waited for Grady to make the slightest nod or noise to indicate: Go on. But Grady couldn't respond. In fact, he wanted desperately to keep

Eli from telling him this, from unburdening his secret heart to him, a stranger he'd never met till tonight and would probably not see again. Grady felt he had to say something, not out of politeness or sympathy, but out of necessity. It seemed to him that a chasm had opened between him and Eli, a hole he must somehow fill before Eli jumped in with the story of his love. The silence reminded him of those hushed moments just before he began his puppet shows, moments he was often tempted to prolong, to see how long they could last—a temptation that always dizzied him with that same mix of fear and seduction he felt on the edge of a cliff.

Eli was getting ready to speak when Grady said, "I used to live in California. In San Francisco. This was ages ago. I was staying with friends. Every night I ate at this Vietnamese greasy spoon down the block. Just a few Formica tables, but they had terrific food. The waitress spoke maybe fifty words of English, but she was so beautiful I didn't care. Pretty soon I noticed I was thinking of her all the time. I began going later each night, imagining how I could ask her to come for a walk after work. I began to notice that when I walked in, she looked strained, as if she was looking for me; then she saw me and her face brightened. So one night we went for a walk up Clement Street. She took me to her room. We got into bed and began kissing. But a funny thing happened. I was nervous. I couldn't . . . ."

"Happens to everyone," Eli said.

"She didn't seem worried," Grady went on. "She got

up and got a letter from a drawer. An aerogram, post-marked Dayton, Ohio. 'Please,' she said, 'read this.' Clearly she meant aloud.

" 'Dear Ba,' I read. 'I love you very much. Every night I go to sleep thinking of what it was like to be with you in Hue. My mother is sick here, so I won't be able to meet your plane when you get into San Francisco. I don't know when I can get there, so here's what to do. Every Saturday, at ten, go to Sutro Park and wait for me. You don't have to wait long. I'll be there the first Saturday after I get into town. I love you. I love you. Tom.'

"I said, 'Do you know what this says?' She smiled and shook her head no. And suddenly I felt I had to make her understand. It was Friday. Tomorrow this guy might be waiting in Sutro Park. 'Come on,' I said, and I took her downstairs where I'd seen some elderly Vietnamese women sitting on the stoop. I found one who spoke English and told her about the letter. She said something in Vietnamese and the girl answered and both of them laughed. The old woman said, 'This is a very old letter. She has already met this boy, she doesn't like him any-more. But she wanted you to read it aloud because she thought it would relax you to tell her a few times, 'I love you.' "

After a silence Eli said, "Wow. What a story. Did it work?"

Grady nodded yes. It was like shaking himself awake. He woke up shocked to find himself here, standing beside Eli, having just told a made-up story about a woman he'd never met, a place he'd never been to, a love affair he'd never had—a story you only had to think about for a second to see it was full of holes.

"How was it?" Eli asked.

It took Grady a moment to realize that Eli meant his night with the Vietnamese girl. He didn't know how to reply. He looked out the window, where now it was so dark that you couldn't see the teenagers, or the snow, couldn't see anything but the glowing green ball and the bright trails it left in the blackness on its high loopy arcs through the air.

"It was amazing," he said.

GHIRLANDAIO

NOT LONG AGO I happened to glance through a book on Renaissance painting. I saw the Ghirlandaio portrait of the old man and his grandson and immediately closed the book. After a while I turned back to the Ghirlandaio, and then I kept looking until, for a moment, I quite forgot where I was. I was remembering the year when that painting was on loan at the museum and my father took me to see it; remembering how, as a child, I couldn't stop staring at the old man in the painting, at his bulbous grapey nose. And I could almost hear my father's voice telling me once again that what the old man had—what made his nose look like that—was lupus erythematosus.

My father was a doctor. He loved medicine and art and loved especially those places where the two seemed to him to coincide: paintings of saints curing lepers; Van Gogh with his digitalis-distorted color sense; Monet, whose retinal degeneration my father pronounced to have influenced his later works; and most of all astigmatic El Greco, his *View of Toledo* that we lingered before, gazing at the roofs and spires and nighttime sky that El Greco with his bad vision had seen and painted as squiggles. My father walked briskly through the museum, visiting his favorites as if he were making hospital rounds, and in my slippery party shoes I skated after him. The Ghirlandaio double portrait was my father's idea of what art should be, and I was glad that it gave him such pleasure, that winter when nothing else did.

I remember that winter so clearly that I can say with both certainty and amazement: I never imagined that by the next year my parents would be divorced. It seems incredible now that they never argued in front of me. But it was also the very last year when I chose to take my parents' word for what was real and what wasn't. I believed life was as they told me, as it seemed, and what seemed to be happening on those Sundays was that my father wanted to go to the museum and my mother didn't, and she argued against his taking me because this was 1955, at the height of the polio scare, and she was afraid I would catch it in the damp overheated galleries.

But polio, my father said, was a summer disease, and besides, the European painting wing wasn't exactly the community swimming pool or a movie theater showing *Dumbo* to a thousand runny-nosed kids. He made it seem silly to worry about this, and only much later did I understand that this was not my mother's real fear. I have often wondered if, at some time on those trips, my father and I might have run into the woman he would soon leave my mother for. How would I have known? She was no one a child would have noticed in a museum full of adults, and even if my father had seen her and reacted, I don't think I would have noticed that either. I was eleven, and the drama of my life was happening elsewhere.

Several times, as we stood before the Ghirlandaio, I asked the same question: "Could someone die from that?" And my father, his love for the subject outweighing his customary awareness of what he had already told me and I had obviously not paid attention to, said, "Well, not immediately." There was a secret conversation beneath this, what he and I knew and did not say: my sixth-grade teacher, Miss Haley, had pretty much the same nose. The reason I kept asking was that—though I couldn't have admitted it, not even to myself—I half hoped Miss Haley might die of it, if not instantly then sometime during the school year.

It is difficult now to remember how large our teachers loomed. Each grade teacher was our fate for a year that lasted so much longer than any year does now; they were the only future we believed in. We collected the rumors, the gossip, the reputations, studied their passions and personality tics for clues to our future happiness. What you heard about Miss Haley was that her nose looked that way because she was a Christian Scientist and wouldn't go to a doctor, and that after a while you got used to it. We heard that you did Ancient Egypt, that she had strong, inexplicable, immutable loves and hates—either she loved or hated you, and you knew which it was right away.

From the first day of school it was perfectly clear that Miss Haley hated me, and sixth grade unrolled before me in all its grim, unendurable length. Miss Haley was a stocky, energetic elderly woman who drew fearlessly on the blackboard in very long straight lines that I recognize only now for the marvels they were. By lunch we felt as if hers were the most normal nose in the world, and we realized the truth of what the former sixth-graders had told us. Something in her presence made it clear that her nose was not to be spoken of—not even among ourselves, in private—and it truly was remarkable, how deeply we took this to heart. We were at an age when we watched very carefully—to see what you said and kept quiet, what you showed and concealed—and this was especially crucial in regard to things of the body.

Many times that first day she repeated, "Of course, when we study Egypt . . ." and she drew an enormous pyramid on the far side of the board. Each day, she explained, one well-behaved student would be called up to write his or her name in a brick. The Good Behavior Pyramid was much too young for sixth grade, when anything that smacked of the babyish embarrassed us beyond words. Even so, I longed—without hope—to write my name in a Good Behavior brick.

Miss Haley's unfriendliness might simply have been the result of that chemical friction that sometimes springs up between teacher and student, so that nothing between them goes right. I was a sallow, skinny girl, alternately know-it-all and mopey—it certainly might have been that. It might have been that I was half Jewish and had a Jewish name in that small, suburban private school where hardly anyone did. Any of that seems more likely now than that Miss Haley disliked me for the reasons I thought—because she and my father (and by extension me) were opposites, because my father represented everything her religion was against, because my father smiled, compassionate and superior, when I told him about her being a Christian Scientist, and because on Sundays my father and I stood before the Ghirlandaio and discussed her disease.

She couldn't have known that, but I imagined she did, and in fact was so certain of it that I never complained to my parents. Enough had begun to seem wrong at home without my adding that. I never suspected the truth—that my father had fallen in love and didn't want to be, and fought it, while my mother waited helplessly for him to decide—no more than I recognized our trips to the museum as almost the only things he could still do for comfort and without guilt. Still I sensed danger, some mood that hung over our breakfasts and dinners, some drifting of attention that made it necessary to repeat what we said to my father several times before he heard. I misread my mother's attempts to charm him and make him laugh, her expecting me to do the same; briefly I worried that my father might be sick, or that he was losing his hearing. And I refused to bring home one more bit of bad tidings for my parents to think was their fault.

I, too, realized the difficulty and great importance of keeping my father interested—but I hesitated to say anything which might accidentally reveal my unhappiness at school. At meals, when my father asked what we were studying, I'd mumble something like "Egypt."

"What about Egypt?" my mother would say.

"I don't know," I'd say. "Pyramids. The Pharaohs."

"What about the pyramids?" said my father.

"I don't know," I'd say.

"*We're* the guys who built the pyramids," he'd say. "Actively *shlepped* the stones." Then catching my mother's eye he'd add, "On my side, that is. On your mother's side, Cleopatra."

Sundays, at the museum, my father often suggested a walk through the Egyptian wing. How it would have pleased him to read me the captions and hear what little I knew. There was so much we could have discussed—embalming techniques, anthrax powder, the ten plagues. But I feared that the artifacts themselves would somehow betray the only information that mattered: I'd never been called on to tell about Osiris being hacked up in chunks and thrown into the Nile, or to make a clay man for the funeral barge our class was constructing, or to fill in, with colored chalk, the scarab Miss Haley outlined each day on the board.

By then our class was launched on what Miss Haley called our little journey down the Nile, and when she pulled the heavy dark-green shades and showed us slides of temples and sarcophagi, I did feel just a bit rocky, as if we were floating past everything that I knew, and the dusty metallic smell of the projector became the salt, garbagey odor of river water and sand. Pretending to watch the slides, I stared at the dust motes streaming in that wedge of light until my eyes went out of focus and the classroom disappeared and a scary chill of aloneness startled me back to myself.

There was no one in whom I could confide; it would have been foolish to let my friends know I cared how much Miss Haley disliked me. We were at that age when much is secret, much is embarrassing, when certain questions—what to do with our shoulders and knees, and whether people like us—assume an intensity they will never have again. At that age, everyone and everything is love object, mirror and judge, and we go around frantically wasting ourselves on whatever is nearby.

On top of my other problems, that year I fell in love. This, too, I had no one to tell. It was one thing to love Elvis—all the girls loved Elvis except a few who were famous for *not* loving Elvis, and there were a couple of upper-school boys we all agreed were cute. But we were late bloomers; love was still something you did in a group, by consensus, and the consensus was that we hated sixth-grade boys.

But there was one I liked. His name was Kenny something. I remember that his last name changed between fifth and sixth grade, when his glamorous actress mother remarried—but I don't remember either name. I have only the fuzziest sense of what he looked like—red hair in a spiky fifties crewcut—which is strange, because our love was so purely physical, so exquisitely located in those angular shoulders and knees, in our skins, in inches of distance between us. All we asked was to look at each other or brush, accidentally, his hip or his elbow grazing me as we ran out to the playground. This happened perhaps twice or three times a week; the rest of the time, I replayed our moment of contact. For days we didn't look at each other. Then a weekend would pass; on Monday the looks and collisions began again. Everything was unspoken, potential, and in constant flux.

Ours was a doomed love. To have acknowledged it, even to each other, would have meant taking on the world—and for what? We might have been forced to have a conversation. In fact, we could barely manage a sentence. My greatest dream and greatest fear was being alone with him, and I liked to terrify myself by imagining occasions on which this might occur. One place where it seemed this might happen was the museum; our class was scheduled to visit the Egyptian wing. For weeks before the trip I invented impossible scenarios of escaping with him into the shadows of the church-like medieval hall that I alone among the sixth-graders knew about. And what would we do then? My mind refused to go further, so I thought it again and again until I came up with a plan to arrange what I wanted and dreaded most.

On the morning of the trip I woke up shaking with fever. I still remember staring down into my dresser drawer, wondering how many sweaters I could get away with wearing. I must have put on three or four, but nothing felt warm. At breakfast, I shivered and tried to hide it. How strange that my parents didn't notice; normally, one sniffle and they were feeling my forehead. But sometime during the night we must have entered that world of mischance that parents so fear, with its history of catastrophes occurring in eye blinks when parental vigilance lapsed.

Briefly I wondered if maybe I did have polio, as my mother so dreaded, but I was still a child, and didn't know what was worth fearing; children rarely fear airplanes but, almost always, the dark. The prospect of missing the trip scared me far more than polio. Besides, I already knew that first principle of everyday magic: once you say something, give it a name, then, only then, can it happen. So I kept quiet and shivered and wrapped my hands around my cocoa cup and everything around me slipped in and out of focus.

This is how I recall that day—at moments the edges of things would be painfully sharp; then they would blur and turn wavy. Kissing my parents goodbye, I was so confused I imagined my father would be interested to hear that the world looked to me like an El Greco painting. But just in time I caught myself and climbed onto the steamed-up bus.

Our classroom was in chaos, but through it all rang Miss Haley's strained voice, yelling, "Hang on to your coats," which struck me as the most deeply kind, the most thoughtful thing she'd ever said. There was one moment, as we lined up to leave, when I knew I was in danger, that I should tell someone and go home. But then I felt someone bump into me, and even through all those sweaters, I knew who it was. Kenny was right behind me in line, and as we pushed toward the narrow bus door, he whispered, "Can we still go see it?" It took me a while to think what he meant, though for days it was all I had thought of.

What he meant was the Ghirlandaio painting, which he'd heard about from me. It had required astonishing bravery to approach him in the schoolyard, to speak to him for so long, but that was minor compared with the courage it took to mention the unmentionable—that is, Miss Haley's nose. I don't recall how I'd phrased it, how precisely I'd made it clear that there existed a work of art with a nose like our sixth-grade teacher's. It had left us both feeling quite short of breath, as if we'd been running and had gotten our second wind and were capable of anything. And in that light-headed state I offered to take him to see it. It would be easy, I said—I knew the museum so well we could sneak off and get back before anyone noticed.

Yet now the idea of walking even the shortest distance exhausted me, and my plan (which I'd never expected him to agree to) seemed to demand impossible stamina —though less than it would have taken to shake my head no. I told him to be on the lookout for the right moment, and my voice dopplered back at me through an echo chamber of fever.

At the museum, a guard instructed us to throw our coats in a rolling canvas bin. And this is my clearest memory from that day—the panic I felt as my coat disappeared, how it looked to me like someone jumping, vanishing into a sea of coats. Suddenly I was so cold I felt I had to keep moving, and I caught Kenny's eye and we edged toward the back of the crowd, and dimly I heard my fever-voice telling him: Follow me.

Not even running helped. I just got colder, wobbly, and unsure; of course we got lost and crisscrossed the damp medieval hall, where the shadows climbed the chill stone walls, pretending to be doorways that vanished when we got close. At last we found the staircase, the right gallery, the Ghirlandaio. And I gloried in the particular pride of having done what I'd boasted I could.

Kenny stared at the painting. Then very softly he said, "Wow. Disgusto."

"Disgusto" was the word, all right. And yet I felt strangely hurt, protective of Ghirlandaio's old man, as if he and his grandson were relatives of mine and Kenny had passed judgment on my family, on my life, on those afternoons when I stood here with my father pretending that this was something compelling and beautiful and not what it was: disgusto.

At that moment we heard footsteps, angry taps on the parquet floor, and we knew whose steps they were, though not how Miss Haley had found us. Instinctively, we moved to the center of the gallery, so no one could tell what painting we'd been near, and I thought—as fast as the fever allowed—that if she noticed the Ghirlandaio, I would direct her eye to the grandson, at how he gazed at the old man, how trustingly and with what love. But she just stood there, glaring at us in the silence of the gallery.

Then Kenny burst into tears. Miss Haley and I looked away from him, embarrassed and upset, though I doubt that she could have been feeling the same emotions that

I was—revulsion, and the strong desire to be anywhere, with anyone but him. Sometimes, in later years, I ran into old loves and wondered what I had seen in them; but that day, in the whirl of eleven-year-old love, this shift of emotion happened instantaneously. The love I had felt just a few hours before now seemed grotesque and absurd. I caught Kenny's smell of hair oil and damp wool, and for a second I gagged.

Was it the tears that so turned me against him? I think it was something more: we were at the age when love cannot stand exposure, when to be caught brings humiliation so profound we can only blame the beloved. We were, in that way, not much older than Adam and Eve, whom we must have resembled as Miss Haley chased us through the galleries, past those paintings of the expulsion from Eden which my father always rushed by—perhaps because the couple was naked or, more likely, held no interest for him, having nothing physically wrong.

Meanwhile, my fever was climbing, the chill in my bones transforming itself into needles of ice. When we rejoined our classmates in the Egyptian wing, I hardly recognized them. Shuffling obediently, gazing morosely at their feet, they could have been the funerary procession that the docent was describing. Miss Haley had prepared us for the highlight of the tour—a trip through the vast Egyptian tomb that the museum had imported brick by brick from Luxor. But as we approached it, the docent narrowed her eyes and dropped her voice to an ominous register and warned us to stay together because the tomb had been built as a maze to foil robbers. And then it hit us all at once—we were entering a grave.

Inside, the temperature dropped. I had never been so cold. Perhaps the docent was chilly, too, or didn't like it there; in any case, she walked faster, until the children were practically trotting to keep up. I knew I couldn't do it—and then the urge to curl up and lie down suddenly overwhelmed me. I let the others push ahead through the twisting corridors, and when we passed a roped-off room, I ducked into it and found a corner where I couldn't be seen from outside.

I crouched in a cul-de-sac, surrounded by glass-covered walls. Beneath the glass were friezes, lit with a soft golden light. Figures in a procession surrounded me. It was a funeral procession, extending into the afterlife to follow the dead and their gods, and it gave me a strange sense of comfort that I knew who everyone was. First came the mourners, shedding their broken-line tears, then the cows, the oxen dragging the carts with all the dead's possessions, then the boats that would ferry them across the waters of the other world. And now came the lesser gods: Bes, the dwarf; Tauret, the hippopotamus; frog-headed Heket; the lioness Renenet; the scorpion Selket.

Slowly the line began to move forward, and I watched it moving across the glassed-in walls like an animated cartoon—the goddess with the balances for weighing the souls of the dead, then Thoth, Isis, Osiris to greet the lucky spirits. And all at once it seemed to me that the figures were leaving the walls and marching straight at me, coming for me and for everyone I loved. In silence came the fifty-two judges, then Horus, Bast, Anubis, the hawk, the cat, the jackal streamed toward me through the air, and at the end of the line stood Amement, the Devourer, crocodile, hippo, lioness, receiver of the souls who had been tried and found guilty.

But really the goddess I saw was Miss Haley, who stood looking down at me, her white hair backlit, flaming around her head. She must have come searching for me, and yet she seemed not to recognize me.

Her face was opaque, her eyes looked visionless and dead, and that seemed strange because it had just occurred to me that I had been wrong, that all this time I had been thinking Miss Haley and I were opposite, when in fact we were just opposite sides of the same coin—she and her Christian Science, me and my father and our Ghirlandaio. We had precisely the same concerns. We did the same things in our spare time. This thought made me strangely, inexplicably happy; I was suffused with affection, not only for Miss Haley but for my father and me, a compassion much deeper than anything we credit children with and so consider the exclusive province of adults. I felt like someone who had solved a hard problem and now could imagine relaxing. I was sleepy and closed my eyes.

It was not, as it happened, polio, but a kind of meningitis that did no lasting damage but kept me in the hospital three months. I came home to two separate houses. Since then I have often wondered why my parents—who were always so careful of me—failed to consider the effect on me of a homecoming like that. Why couldn't they have waited? But I think that they must have considered waiting and found that they had no choice.

My father and I were never so close again. For a long while I was angry at him, and somewhere in that time stopped wanting to please him and tell him interesting things, including something I remembered, a thought I had but couldn't say when he came to pick me up at the museum.

I remember very clearly lying on a cot in a room with adults gathered around. I looked up and saw my father's face, all wavy and distorted and extraordinarily beautiful, and I wanted to tell him something but couldn't speak, wanted to say it so badly that I can remember it now.

What I wanted to say was this: that he had been wrong about El Greco, that if something was straight and you saw it curved, you would actually paint it straight; your hand would correct what your eye had seen wrong, so it finally came out right. Then the objects in your painting would appear to you just as everything always did—distorted, buckled, and curved. But anyone else who looked at it would see what you never saw—a perfect likeness of the world, the world as it really was.

AMATEUR
VOODOO

PHILIP ASKS for paper, crayons, and tape, and papers his bedroom walls with drawings of cats. He's trying to work magic, to bring his cat back home. It's been four days since he and his parents returned from Cape Cod to find Geronimo gone. Philip and Frank and Jenny took turns calling the cat, and then, when it got dark, Philip sat on the front steps with a flashlight and an open cat-food can.

"Amateur voodoo," says Frank. Basically Frank approves; some part of him even thinks it might work. In that way he and Philip are different from Jenny, who, from the start, assumed the cat was gone for good.

Philip hasn't mentioned Geronimo since that first night, and even when he takes Jenny upstairs to see his room, she senses that he still doesn't want to talk about it. He has used maybe fifty sheets from the reams of Xerox paper they buy him. Every picture is different. Cat close-ups and long shots, cats that are all whiskers and others doing things like riding bikes. Later, Frank says, "He's got his room done like Lourdes." But Jenny has had another kind of flash: those little Mexican statues of skeletons playing volleyball, riding bikes, doing just what Philip's cats are, and with similar crazy smiles.

Both of them think this is basically good, this evidence in Philip of loyalty and love. Jenny just wonders: good for whom? On their vacation, Philip, who is six, fell in love with a fifteen-year-old girl. Cheryl's parents were renting the house next door; there were no other kids around. She and Philip would go to the beach. Jenny and Frank weren't surprised—Philip is better company than most adults. Free babysitting, they thought. But then a sixteen-year-old boy showed up and Cheryl went off with him. Philip said he was sleepy and wouldn't come out of his room, and they realized that it had been—in every way but one, they hoped—just like an adult love. It shadowed everything for a day or so, until Philip cheered up. Things must be in proportion if Philip is working harder to get back his cat than he did to get back Cheryl, though maybe it just seems to him more possible.

Already this cat has had a fairly complicated history. Philip got him in May, as a kitten. A friend found him on her lawn; a passing car must have left him there. Well, not a friend, exactly; a woman named Ada whom Frank was in love with for two very terrible months. That was four years ago. At that time, Jenny had felt certain that she and Frank couldn't go on; now she is shocked by how much she has—or mostly has—forgotten. Ada has half moved back into Boston; they rarely see her. They hadn't seen her at all this spring till the pond— directly across the road from her driveway—was blown up.

Pedersen's pond was where everyone used to go. When they first moved to New Hampshire, ten years ago, the pond was where they found each other, couple by couple and one by one. They swam there as young people with bodies pretty enough for skinny-dipping, then as mothers bringing their children to play, even after some of them could have afforded to put in ponds of their own. It had never been safe—no lifeguard, slippery banks—but they were careful. Sometimes swimmers had to be dragged in to shore; Frank used to ride with the rescue squad, and several times he was called out there to make sure some drunken teenager was okay. But no one ever really got hurt, no one ever drowned.

This year Pedersen's insurance carrier scared him about liability. He dynamited the pond at 5 A.M., with a crew he'd brought in from North Conway.

Word got out, and everyone made a kind of pilgrimage. Even Frank and Jenny, who hadn't swum there in several summers, felt they had to see. It looked like the set of a big-budget war movie. Uprooted spruces lay ten feet from the ragged holes they'd come out of; the blasting had destroyed a large section of the woods. You'd have thought a former pond would be mucky, but the water had drained away fast. There was just a scarred empty flat space where the deep part used to be. Everything was dried out; the leaves looked ripped and brown with dust —grimy, like unwashed cars. Philip had mixed feelings about the pond; he'd grown a little afraid of the water, while most of his friends had already learned to swim. But Philip, too, seemed stunned.

Then they saw Ada walking across the road. Even in her bare feet, Ada always seemed to be wearing high heels. She was carrying something against her shoulder, a taffy-colored kitten. As she got closer, Jenny and Frank found it easiest to look at the cat. Ada looked down at it, too; then everyone focused on Philip, who was staring at the kitten. He graced Ada with his shy, six-year-old James Dean smile. "Hey," he said. "Nice cat."

"Someone drop him off on my lawn," Ada said. Ada is Czech, but everyone who meets her thinks she is French. She has been in this country fifteen years, but holds on to her accent and her own sense of English grammar and word order.

It took Jenny a moment to figure out that she was talking about how she'd gotten the cat. Frank understood right away.

"Take it," said Ada. "Please. It and the baby, already they know each other. Maybe from some other life."

Philip kept silent and let himself be called a baby. Jenny and Frank took turns saying, "We can't." Then almost in unison, they said, "Well, why not?" And everyone started to laugh. Ada said, "Come in. Think about it. Have tea."

Jenny said, "Thanks, we can't." She said, "I mean, about tea. It's all right. We'll take the cat."

They talked for a few more moments. Jenny asked about Jan, Ada's husband, who is a surgeon and rarely comes out from Boston, about Milan and Eva, their nearly grown children; everyone was fine. Ada asked about the winter: had it been bad?

"We survived," Philip said.

"What winter?" said Jenny. "I can't remember."

No one mentioned Pedersen's pond.

On the way home, Jenny said, "I'll bet we wouldn't have taken the cat if we hadn't just seen what they did to the pond. We needed to make some gesture in the face of that."

Frank said, "That cat is one lucky duck." If anyone else had given them the kitten, he thought, in a week or two he would call to report on its progress. He didn't think he would call Ada.

They had all enjoyed feeling big—adult, sensible, forgiving. Leaving Ada's, Jenny had said, "I'm glad it worked out." She meant the instant and clearly mutual affection between Philip and the cat. That Jenny would permit him to take a cat from Ada showed how much time had passed. It would have *meant* something to refuse.

Philip named the cat. When it was tiny, he used to throw it up in the air and yell, "Geronimo!" He never threw it hard. Only once Jenny saw the kitten stumbling off looking dazed, and Philip snatched it up and kissed it and said, "I'm sorry."

What makes Jenny feel pessimistic now is a note from the high-school kid they paid to feed Geronimo while they were gone. The note said, "No cat since Tuesday. I called and called." Philip—who is learning to read—can't decipher that reckless high-school scrawl, and Jenny doesn't tell him. Frank says, "The cat'll be back." They've all grown fond of Geronimo. They want to believe Frank is right.

The cat has been gone eight days—not four, as Philip believes—when Philip papers his room with drawings of cats, and Frank asks Jenny to come with him to the neighbor. That either of them should suggest this is a sign of how much is at stake.

In the five years since the new house went up on the land bordering theirs, they have talked to the neighbor just twice; once, when the foundation was being put in, they asked if it couldn't be dug somewhere else—anywhere on the neighbor's fifty acres where they wouldn't see it from their kitchen window; and once, across a table at a friend's dinner party, when they really had no choice.

At first there was much ill will—they wouldn't acknowledge the neighbor on the road, pretended not to see him in the store or the bank. But that only increased his importance, his claim on their lives, so now they nod and wave. And when Jenny looks out of her kitchen window his house doesn't register, is not there, is hidden behind some psychic equivalent of an optical blind spot.

The neighbor (they never speak or think of him as anything but "the neighbor") is a biologist. They tried to see this as a comfort—it could have been a rod-and-gun club next door—until he partly filled in the wetland behind his house to alleviate a drainage problem; herons used to wade there, and in spring, huge flocks of geese would stop on their way to wherever.

The neighbor had a wife when he moved here. Her name was Mercedes. For a while the wind used to carry the sound of them yelling. She was gone by the time of that dinner party—moved to New York, said the gossip. Jenny has often thought that all the resentment they'd focused on the neighbor's house must have had its effect.

In fact, it's probably true that their real-estate feud didn't help his domestic life. If things were as bad as they sounded, his wife probably took their side.

The neighbor's cat, a glossy gray-and-white male, has always felt free to walk on Frank and Jenny's lawn. At first it made Jenny shudder, like a possum or a wood-chuck, something you wouldn't kill but you didn't have to like. But finally she and Frank had to admit: it was a pretty cat. It seems possible that at some lonely dinner hour Geronimo went to eat with the neighbor's cat, though they tell themselves that Geronimo would be home by now, wouldn't stay there after they'd come back.

They wait until Philip is in day camp. If what's hap-pened is what Jenny secretly suspects—that the neighbor has run the cat over in his driveway—they would like to predigest the news and tell Philip themselves.

The neighbor answers the door in tennis shorts and a T-shirt. If it were anyone else, Jenny would think he had a handsome, well-cared-for body, but in this case she thinks: Imagine, a guy living alone and keeping his shorts and T-shirts so white.

Jenny makes Frank let *her* talk; she is less likely, she says, to let all the events of those first few months make the most casual question tense and malignant with strain. She says, "Listen, have you seen a little taffy-colored cat?"

The neighbor claps his hand over his mouth. He says, "Oh, my God, that was yours?" He says the cat was around. He says it was fighting with his cat, and besides, he couldn't feed another cat, and just at that moment the gray-and-white cat shows up, as if it knows they are discussing it. The neighbor says he's sorry, he took the little cat and drove it down the road and left it in a field at the very bottom of Cider Hill Road. He thought it could catch mice there.

Frank and Jenny look at each other and roll their eyes. Otherwise, they feel eerily calm. Frank says, "You must be joking." Jenny says, "That was our cat." Her voice sounds thin and slightly whiny, like Philip protesting some irrevocable adult decision. The neighbor says, "I'm sorry, I'm really, really sorry." Neither Frank nor Jenny says anything to that. With shrugs and neutral gestures expressing something halfway between "Don't be" and "You should be," they turn and leave. The neighbor calls after them, "Hey, man, I'm really sorry."

Frank says, "Can you believe he told us? If *I* did that, I would *never* have told. I would have said, 'What cat? I didn't see any cat.' "

"You wouldn't have done it," says Jenny.

They are home drinking coffee when Jenny finally says, "Of course the truly strange thing is that he should have dropped it off on Cider Hill Road." That is where Ada lives, where they got Geronimo in the first place, although the field the neighbor means is miles from Ada's house. "Does he know Ada?"

"I doubt it," says Frank.

"Oh, I don't know," Jenny says. "Maybe that cat just wasn't meant to be our cat. Maybe we should leave it."

"It's Philip's cat," says Frank.

Frank says he'll go to Cider Hill and look for the cat. He'll go after Philip comes home from camp, this evening, after dinner. He'll take Philip with him.

"I'll go with you," Jenny says.

Later, as they are getting into the car, Philip says, "Wouldn't it be weird if the cat turned up at Ada's?" Of course they are all thinking that. Philip knows only that Ada is a fairly distant family friend. It irritates Jenny that her son should just say Ada's name as if it were perfectly normal.

Frank is driving, and as they turn up Cider Hill Road, Jenny has one of those moments of clarity and prescience: she is positive that the cat is at Ada's. For an instant it crosses her mind that the neighbor has met Ada, knows their histories, that this is at once their retribution and his revenge. But it all seems unlikely—hardly anyone knew about Ada and Frank. Even if the neighbor knew everything—whose cat it was and where it came from and all they had gone through—he wasn't the type to even let himself consider revenge.

They stop at the first house on the road, nearest the field the neighbor described. Frank is acquainted with the old couple who live there. He sends Philip up to the door, and Philip comes back beaming. "They saw him," says Philip, and points farther on down the road.

From what they can tell, the cat has made its way along the road, dining at a different home every night. Everyone seems to have been struck by its winning personality. Jenny counts the houses, the nights the cat's been gone, and remembers the counting games she played as a child: how far in advance you could see you'd be "out." The cat is at Ada's, there's no doubt in her mind, but still for the sake of form they keep stopping at houses, tracing the cat's progressive dinner up the hill.

Ada lives in a white frame eyebrow colonial up a long drive surrounded by trees; when you get out of the car in the clearing in front of the house, you feel you are being watched. It makes Jenny wonder who would drop off a cat back here. Though Ada says some outrageous things, she has never actually lied.

Three cats play in front of the house, but Geronimo isn't among them. Frank, Jenny, and Philip walk up the steps; it's Philip who knocks on the door. No one answers, but Geronimo appears at the window, pressing his face on the glass. Philip jumps up to meet him. Frank steps up and knocks. No one answers. Frank says, "We can't just go in and get it." Philip says, "Isn't it strange that it's here?"

"*Strange* is the word," says his father.

Finally Ada appears. She is wearing a beautiful antique silk kimono. Her hair is down on her forehead, and she pushes it back with her hand. "I am just sleeping," she says. "Jan is in Boston." But Philip has already pushed by her and is hugging the cat.

"How the cat came here?" Ada says.

Frank seems on the point of telling the story, but something stops him. Instead, he looks at Jenny, who tells the story quickly, emphasizing the neighbor's villainy. Ada makes clicking sounds and says, "How terrible. How awful. Oh, what a terrible man." There is a silence. Then Ada says, "Him you never liked. I come home, I don't know why the cat is here. I think it don't work out with you, and maybe you drop her here when I am gone."

"We wouldn't do that," Jenny says.

There's another pause, and Ada sighs. "Well, it could have been sad but is happy. And now you have to come in."

Ada steps aside to let Frank and Jenny pass. They follow her into the kitchen. Ada's kimono, and Ada herself, makes it impossible not to notice the body under the silk. Frank is struck—as if for the first time—by how much civilization depends on not seeing certain things and pretending others never occurred. Jenny notices, too, and tries not to see. The only way she survived that time and forgave and kept going was by refusing to let certain pictures enter her head. She and Frank sit down across from each other at the pine kitchen table.

"This time we drink to the cat," Ada says. "We drink to it staying home with you where it belongs." She takes out three delicate shot glasses with deep blue rims and plunks them on the table with a bottle of vodka from the freezer. She and Frank and Jenny clink glasses and drink. No one looks at anyone else. Ada says, "You have been again to the pond?"

Frank says, "What a mess." And suddenly Jenny is surprised by a strange feeling: she's glad that the pond is gone. But why should that surprise her? The night every-thing started between Frank and Ada, Jenny had been in Boston, visiting a friend, and when she got back everyone in the grocery was talking about the drunken teenage kid the rescue squad saved from drowning in Pedersen's pond. But Frank hadn't told her, hadn't mentioned it, and when she asked him, he looked guilty and said, "What kid?" She had seen Frank and Ada talking at parties; it had made her unhappy. And right then she knew—just as she knew today that the cat would be back at Ada's—she knew that Frank had gone over to Ada's when he got through at the pond.

Suddenly Jenny feels panicked. She wants to get Philip and Frank and get out. She feels she cannot stand it that the memory of that night is something that Frank and Ada share, and it is different from hers. What she does not know, or want to know, is this:

That night, when Ada opened her door and saw Frank, she burst into tears. When at last she stopped crying and pacing and smoking cigarettes, she told him that she had wanted to see him so badly, she had been almost hoping that something would happen at the pond, that he would have to go there and he would be so close to her house, and he would know she wanted to see him, he would have felt it, and that night he would stop by. When she had heard the sirens and cars, she couldn't help thinking she'd caused it. But still she prayed Frank would come. Frank said she couldn't have caused it. And besides, the kid was all right.

Amateur Voodoo

There is a long silence. No one seems able to speak. They finish their vodka and Ada pours another round. Then Ada says, "Look. The sky." Outside, the clouds have turned lavender. Ada and Frank and Jenny gaze fixedly out the window; it is something that's easy to stare at with more interest than they feel.

Suddenly a voice says, very clearly, "Did you miss me?" And all three of them turn, a little fast, a bit startled— as if they don't know that it's Philip, murmuring to his cat.

POTATO

WORLD

ALL SPRING I WAITED for something to save me from working that summer. That was how I wound up at Potato World. A sixtyish Frenchwoman named Yvette owned the franchise at the mall. She interviewed me for two seconds and said, "You are my new sous-chef!" My job was to scrub the potatoes and preroast them in the microwave. Ronnie, the counterman, finished them off with the customer's choice of topping. I was shocked by how many people ordered ratatouille-stuffed baked potatoes; maybe that was because I'd seen the industrial-size ratatouille cans.

Yvette came in at the end of the day to empty the cash register. Otherwise, Ronnie and I were pretty much on our own. Ronnie had a double mohawk: two parallel brushes down his scalp, like a tool for de-icing car windows. When I asked him what the color was called, Ronnie said, "Fiberglass pink."

Ronnie wore two thin copper bracelets to block the toxins in the potatoes from creeping up his arms. I often wanted to borrow them, but I was embarrassed to ask. The potatoes came in fifty-pound sacks, and each time I reached in, clouds of powdery dirt and pesticide puffed up into my face.

Around lunchtime my boyfriend, Jason, came in, his face still messy from sleep. He and Ronnie and I smoked dope in the back of the kitchen. Jason said, *"I'll* say potato world. This whole town is potato world."

"Potato planet," said Ronnie.

We had a phone near the cash register that no one ever called in on. So when it rang in the morning, I'd know it was Jason for me. He called on his bedroom phone; he was working on his dreams. He claimed this was his summer job; his mother and father were rich. Jason was into the Iroquois, who told the whole clan their dreams, and an African tribe who encouraged you to go back into your dream and face the tiger that woke you the last time. Jason was experimenting with dream communication; he'd tell me what he'd dreamed and ask if the images matched anything I'd been thinking that morning. His idea was to program himself to dream about eco-disaster and nuclear strikes and then he would dream through them and wake up with a solution. I closed my eyes and let his voice stream over me like rain. I said, "Will you still like me when I turn into a potato?"

He said, "There isn't time for that. We'll be back in school before then." As we talked on the phone, I studied the sign above the counter, hand-in-hand smiley international potatoes in serapes and coolie hats. This was definitely not my idea of what a potato was. I was becoming increasingly weird about the potato sacks. There was something about the powderiness, the darkness deep inside—half the time I was positive I'd reach down there and grab a rat.

One afternoon I was steeling myself for a dip into the potatoes when I heard a familiar voice order a giant fries. I looked around and said, "You might want to rethink that." Though my father looked young and trim, he'd had a giant heart attack. Ronnie looked puzzled until I said, "Relax, it's only my dad."

"Who's My Little Pony?" my father whispered when Ronnie turned his back.

I said, "His name is Ronnie. We're engaged. You're not invited to the wedding. What are you doing here?" Though we talked sometimes on the telephone, I hadn't seen him in weeks.

He said, "I've come to lift you up and over Potato World."

I said, "Go ahead. Try it. Lift me."

My father said, "The choice is clear. Potato World or Paris."

When I got home that night my mother said, "Oh, thank God you're safe."

I said, "Why wouldn't I be?"

My mother said, "This morning going to work I was walking down Tenth Street, I saw something strange in the middle of the block, at first it looked like one of those pottery chicken cookie jars, then maybe a stuffed chicken, but when I got close I saw it was a live chicken, on the pavement against a building, hardly moving, just blinking very slowly, like it was in some kind of coma, and then I saw that all its tail feathers were off and I thought, This chicken's been sexually abused, and I felt this cold chill like something awful was going to happen and naturally I've been worried all day that it would happen to you. That mall is full of serial killers."

I thought: No wonder I can't grab a potato without expecting rat teeth. I said, "I'm not surprised. You should see the awful shit they fry up at Beak 'n Biscuit."

My mother said, "Don't say shit."

I said, "Guess who came in today."

My mother said, "Charlie Manson."

I said, "Close. Try: Dad."

My mother said, "Perfect. The class place to bring your teenage sweethearts. What's he down to now? Nineteen?"

I said, "He was alone. He wants me to go to Paris with him."

My mother was silent. Then she said, "A woman in my office just got back from Paris. She got dysentery from couscous."

I said, "Be reasonable. Paris isn't Casablanca."

She said, "Believe it or not, it cheers me up that you know the word Casablanca." She said, "I wish you wouldn't go." Then she said, "When are you leaving?"

Yvette said, "Oh, Par-ee." She seemed so excited I asked if she was from there. She said, "No, we are not." Only then did it dawn on her what this meant for her. She and Ronnie exchanged quick looks, like parents I'd disappointed. I said, "It's only Monday. I can work through Friday night."

The next day Ronnie said, "I'm with you. Another week or two here and I'm potato history."

I said, "Ronnie, you can do better than this. You're really smart. I mean it."

He said, "Don't buy a leather jacket there. They're all American-made. They export $149 cheesy mall pieces of shit, and they get these retarded French kids to buy them for fifteen hundred bucks."

I stared dumbly at Ronnie. I couldn't do the arithmetic. I said, "I didn't sleep last night."

Ronnie said, "You look it."

I'd been arguing with Jason, he'd driven somewhere in the country and we'd sat in his car. Finally, all I could think about was how frantic my mother must be, so we went home and continued it on the phone all night. We kept repeating ourselves. I'd say, "What would *you* pick: three weeks in Europe or three weeks scrubbing potatoes?" He'd say, "How would *you* feel: your girlfriend just disappears." Asking each other to imagine being us made it clear that we weren't each other, though there had been moments that spring and summer when it had seemed that we were.

When I called Jason to say goodbye, he said, "Fine. Don't blame *me*."

We sat three across on the airplane, my father, Robin, and I. My father had introduced us at the airport. He said, "Robin joined the firm around the start of last year. The guys whose heads we brought her in over are totally pissed off."

Robin was tiny and startled-looking with spiky stand-up blond hair that didn't quite go with her business suit and $200 high heels. As soon as the no-smoking light went off, Robin pulled down her tray, perhaps to hide what I'd noticed before: her hands just shook and shook. Her fingernails were airbrushed with swirls, top-of-the-line Korean. At least Robin wasn't twenty, my father's favorite age. He could let her be older than usual; she was smaller and more afraid.

When Robin went to smoke a cigarette, I said, "She reminds me a little of Mom."

He said, "Do you know how long it would have taken me to talk your mother onto this plane? Everything just got to be too goddamn labor-intensive."

Robin ate the high-cholesterol stuff off my father's food tray—quietly, efficiently, she just vacuumed it up. She said, "I have an insane metab," and her hand shot up like a rocket. She said, "Obviously, so do you," and then, "I'm sorry. Don't you hate it when strangers act like they know about you? I mean, about your metabolism."

I said, "What's your job, exactly?" My father was in advertising; he'd done the ad with the conga line of pine-apples with little Carmen Mirandas on their heads. Now he was going over to tell the French how to make the American consumer stop associating mustard with hot dogs.

"I'm a lawyer," Robin said, "I can't believe it, either."

"She's my translator," said my father. "She grew up in Quebec."

"What translator?" said Robin. "The mustard people speak English."

The movie was *Fatal Attraction*, which all of us had seen, a funny choice for them to show—there were little kids on the plane. Robin watched without the sound. My father read. I fell asleep. I had a dream about Jason. It was a kind of erotic, melting dream though nothing sexual happened. The general feeling of the dream was like getting a suntan.

On the expressway into the city, I fell asleep again. I woke up thinking that I was back home and that I'd missed the whole trip. It took me a while to focus and see the French traffic streaming around us.

The air in Paris was like airport air, complete with the fuel-oil smell. Walking outside was like being stuck behind a fucked-up Rabbit diesel. Hot as it was, all the kids wore leather, just like Ronnie had said. All I had were jeans and Jason's big men's shirts. I'd told Jason, "I couldn't find someone else. I'll be wearing your clothes."

My father and Robin were out all day. I slept till eleven. I liked the empty garden café on the hotel roof where I could spend an hour over breakfast and sign for coffee and croissants. I got a map, I walked miles, I took the Métro, it was easy. I went to Notre Dame and the Louvre. Afterwards I sat in the park and imagined a letter to Jason. "Today," it said, "I saw a museum of Japanese tourist haircuts."

The next day I went to the Cluny Museum. There was almost no one there, except one punk girl near the carved stone tombs with the stone people lying on top. It was cool and quiet, with a damp cavey smell I liked. I began to go there every day as if it were a job. I sat with my back against the stones and wrote letters in my head. I went over every word until I had it perfect. I wrote Jason that when I closed my eyes I felt totally medieval; the world got slower and colder till it dropped off the edge of my brain. I hallucinated a chorus of monks, singing solemn hymns. It gave me a yawning, wide-open feeling, like after a shower or sex. The outside seemed to disappear, the cafés I'd had to pass, the tables of kids and glamorous grownups leading cool lives without me in them.

Sometimes I'd go to cafés and order by pointing at people's drinks. The green ones tasted like mouthwash, the brown like herbal cancer cures. I hoped someone would join me, even a scary Moroccan. I felt I could handle anything because I didn't know French.

One day two Haitian guys sat down, Jean Luc and Baptiste. They were young and pretty and had big Rasta hair. Jean Luc wore a flowing white shirt and pants and wanted to be a designer. Baptiste spoke the most English; he was a musician. Jean Luc commented on the passersby—he could tell where everyone got their clothes and exactly how much they'd paid—and Baptiste translated for me.

When two policemen walked by, Baptiste said, "You must be very careful." Then he told me a story about a girl they knew who'd been picked up by two gendarmes and taken for a ride and forced to give one cop a blow job, but she was smart, she had a paper cup in her purse, and after they let her go she spit the cop's come in the cup and brought it in for protein analysis and the cop got busted. All this was surprisingly easy to say in Baptiste's bad English. He asked me if things like this ever happened at home. I asked why she had a cup. Baptiste translated for Jean Luc and they looked at me and shrugged. "Be careful," they told me when I left. I smiled and said I would.

I went back to the hotel and watched a soap opera in French. The camera ping-ponged back and forth between an arguing man and woman. I went out of focus and fell asleep and had another dream. I dreamed Jason and I were in his bed; his parents were off at work. In my dream I kept waking up and going back into the dream.

Finally Robin woke me, knocking on my door. She asked if I wanted to come next door and have a drink with them.

My father had his jacket off. He was lying on the bed, his head propped up at the very same angle it always had at home. Seeing him, it was as if nothing had changed, or everything were interchangeable, Robin and my mother, Dan Rather and the news in a language I didn't understand. I wondered: If I went back to sleep, would I dream about Jason again?

Robin took off her heels and put on enormous furry brown slippers with plastic claws, like a bear's. "From the Anchorage airport," she said. "I take them every-where. I'm terrified of flying."

My father said, "Jesus, it's only an hour till we have to go out again." To me he said, "You might *like* seeing a bunch of squeaky-clean French mustard yuppies."

"What kind of restaurant?" I said, though I had no

intention of going. "Trendy couscous," said Robin. "Isn't that insane?"

The minute they left I went back to my room and lay down and turned off the lights. I concentrated on Jason and got into my dream. Though maybe I should have done something healthy, gone out with my father and Robin, because now the dream changed, and Jason and I were the French TV fighting soap-opera couple. Only this time I knew what the argument was about: he had found someone else. There were no events in this dream either, it was only a feeling—as if the world were turning its back, shutting like a clam. I woke up sad and furious and reached for the phone.

Jason and I had both had dreams in which the other person betrayed us. But it was completely different when you woke with the person beside you, or reachable by telephone, a local call away. I gave the operator Jason's number. I didn't care what time it was, he had his own phone. It rang twice and he answered. I said, "I had one of those horrible dreams, you left me for someone else."

He said, "This is really incredible. You won't believe how incredible this is."

I said, "Come on. Is it true?"

He said, "Later. We'll talk about it later. I can't deal with anything this incredible right now."

I said we wouldn't talk about it later or ever, I didn't want to be with him, no second chances on this one. We broke up over the phone. I hung up and after a while it rang. I let it keep on ringing. Then I called downstairs and told the clerk to please hold my incoming calls.

The next day I realized I'd been processing Paris, shredding it up and spitting out mental letters to Jason. When I wasn't writing to him in my head I didn't know where to look. I don't remember that day very well. Maybe I went shopping. I couldn't do francs into dollars or tell if what I was seeing cost sixty or six hundred. I went out and I came back. I didn't buy anything. The light on my phone was blinking. I wished I hadn't gone out. If I'd been here I could have answered but I couldn't call Jason back. When I called down they said my mother had phoned: call home no matter how late.

I said, "Hi, what time is it there? Did I wake you up?"

"I don't know," my mother said. "Is everything okay?"

"Fine," I said. "What's up?"

"It's Jason," said my mother. "He broke into our house."

I had visions of really embarrassing things, like him stealing my underwear.

"He dyed his hair," my mother said. "In our bathroom sink. Brown," she said. "Like his father. You'll see when he shows up."

Apparently Jason had stolen his father's passport and spare eyeglasses and dyed his hair like his father's and charged a one-way ticket to Paris on his mother's MasterCard. Everyone was positive he was coming to see me, but the jury was still out on why he'd needed our

bathroom sink. My mother said, "What's with you two?"
I said, "I guess he must miss me."

I put down the telephone and waited to feel excited.
But all I felt was embarrassment in advance, like when
someone from one part of your life is about to show up
in another. I knew that sleeping all day in a Paris hotel
room so I'd dream about my boyfriend was a fairly pitiful
excuse for a private world, but so what, it was my world,
I had it to myself. I ordered a Coke from room service
and double-locked the door. I felt like I was wanted by
the F.B.I.

That night I went to dinner with just my father and
Robin. I made her come to the bathroom with me and
told her on the way—just the part about Jason stealing
stuff and being headed here. I could tell she was im-
pressed that a boy would do that for me. She stopped
right by someone's table and asked what I planned to do.
"I don't know," I told her. "Just don't tell my dad."

Unlocking my door, I got a chill that Jason was already
there, the same chill that I used to feel reaching into the
potatoes. I thanked God for the light, the covers turned
back, the little chocolate on my pillow. I lay down and
thought about Jason. I wanted a dream in which it was
warm and we were happy together, a dream from which
I would wake not caring if he'd dyed his hair fiberglass
pink. But I had the wrong kind of dream; in fact, the
wrong kind of sex dream. I dreamed that Jason and some
strange girl were naked in his bed. The creepy and per-
verted part was that I sort of liked watching. I thought

about the Iroquois, how terrible it must be to live where everyone hears your dreams, and one night you have the kind of dream you could never tell anyone ever.

When I woke it was daylight. I knew that it was Jason pounding on the door. I said, "How did you get here so fast? What happened to your head?"

The top inch of his forehead was a root-beer brown, with a hard edge like a bathtub ring bleeding down from his hair. "I don't know what went wrong," he said. "Anyway, I'm sorry."

I said, "Doesn't it wash out?" Then I said, "Who was it?"

"Well," he said, "it was Nan."

I said, "You're kidding. That hog." I couldn't help seeing Jason and Nan, his body wrapped around hers, only now it wasn't like my dream, not interesting but repulsive; sex seemed like a truly disgusting thing for two people to do. I thought of some little details I hadn't liked about Jason, how sunken and white his chest was, a certain way he touched me that he didn't know hurt. Sometimes when we were together I'd think about these things, and it was funny how they moved me, made me love him more. But I didn't like thinking about them now, I was happy how bad his hair looked. I said, "This would be totally different if you hadn't fucked somebody else."

"It was nothing," he said. "I was mad at you."

"It was not nothing," I said.

He said, "I thought you'd believe me if I came and said it in person."

I would have died if someone had come down the hall right then. "You'd better come in," I said.

Jason sat on the edge of the bed. "I don't have a passport," he said. "I was trying to cash a check at the bank and the teller got suspicious. She went off to get someone, and I just turned and split. She had my passport and traveler's checks. I'll bet I'm wanted by the cops."

"I can't imagine how they'll find you," I said. "The guy with the two-tone forehead. Is that how you left my mom's sink?"

"Please don't be angry," he said. "Everything will be all right if I can just sleep for a while."

"Great," I said. "A great idea. I'll be back around dinner."

I went out and walked around. It was totally hot and polluted. I almost couldn't bear it that Jason was back in my room. I felt like the world was a TV screen he was standing directly in front of. It completely skipped my mind that I had been lonely before; I felt as if I had friends in Paris that he wouldn't let me see. I sat on the stones at the Cluny and thought about my father, that the way I felt about Jason now was how he'd thought of my mother and me.

That made me feel instantly guilty and I went back to the hotel; this lasted until I saw Jason had got hair dye on my pillows. He said, "Jesus, I'm starving." I said we could chance the roof café, and he fell back asleep. I was beginning to worry that the dye had bled through to his brain when he woke and got out of bed and raced me to the door. He wouldn't have dared to tell me if he'd had a dream.

Waiting for the elevator, I noticed it was evening. I wondered where the day had gone, where my father and Robin were. The roof café was different at night, crowded with glittery people. The twinkly lights of Paris looked like restaurant design. We didn't have reservations; there were no empty tables. Just as we were getting ready to leave, I saw Robin sitting alone.

Robin seemed glad to see me. She looked half blotto, but nervous blotto, talky and high-strung. "I'm hiding out," she said. "He's driving me nuts. He watches over me like I'm about to vanish off the face of the earth, and the thing is, *I* always think I'm about to disappear, and when he's around and he's thinking it, too, I get so I almost believe it."

"Disappear how?" I said.

"Oh, I don't know," said Robin. "Vanish, vaporize maybe. Spontaneously combust. I'm sorry, I'm so sorry, I keep forgetting he's your dad. He's downstairs. He's fine. He's sleeping."

Jason said, "*I* was sleeping."

Robin and I stared at him as if he'd just appeared. "This is Jason," I said.

"Do you mind if I ask," said Robin, "what you did to your head?"

"Hair dye," Jason said.

"Serious fashion mistake," Robin said. "Something's got to work on that. Kerosene? Nail-polish remover?"

Jason said, "I think I'd like to wait awhile before I give my head a toxic bath."

"It's all a toxic bath," said Robin. "Have you seen the moon?"

Well, I couldn't imagine how we could have missed it. The moon was gigantic, nearly full, half hidden behind a cloud, looming like another huge head just behind Jason's right ear. Maybe the reason we'd missed it was: it was a frightening color. Actually, maybe we'd seen it and blocked it—it was kind of brown.

"This is worse than New *Jersey*," said Robin. "At least there you still get that great industrial orange."

"It looks like a potato," said Jason. "The whole world's a fucking tuber. Mondo Potato. Right?"

Robin leaned very close to him and took his forearm in both hands. "It's all right," she said slowly. "Or it will be all right."

It bothered me for a second that she didn't even know him and he was the one whose arm she was grabbing, pumping with sympathy. But why should that have surprised me? He was the one who deserved it, whose heart was being broken. He was the one whose story this was, the one who would get to tell about his first love and how it ended, how he made a mistake, dyed his hair, stole his father's passport, went to Paris to find his true love, and lost her anyway. We were dividing everything;

all of this was now his. From now on, whatever happened would happen to one of us at a time.

Robin said, "You know what I wonder? If the earth looks like a potato, too, if it looks like Mr. Potato Head when you see it from the moon. And the moon sees everything on earth like potato skin—potato ears and cracks and dirt, scaly spots on the peel."

"The potato pyramids," said Jason. "The potato Grand Canyon."

I looked out at the lights of Paris and the traffic rushing beneath. When I closed my eyes the city noise sounded like waves on shore. I pictured one of those photos from space, I imagined rocketing off, the awe and homesickness of seeing Earth come up in your rearview mirror. I felt something cold rush past my cheek, a comet turning to ice. "The potato Eiffel Tower," I said. "The potato Great Wall of China."

DOG

STORIES

SO OFTEN, AT WEDDINGS, one kisses and hugs the bride and groom and then stands there dumbstruck, grinning with dread. But today the guests congratulate Christine and John and immediately ask Christine, "How's your leg?" If Christine's leg didn't hurt, she might almost feel thankful that a dog bit her a few days ago and gave her guests something to say.

Hardly anyone waits for an answer. They can see for themselves that Christine is wearing a bandage but limping only slightly. They rush on with the conversation, asking, "What happened, exactly?" though nearly all of them live nearby, and nearly all of them know.

By now Christine can tell the story and at the same time scan the lawn to see who has come and who hasn't, to make sure someone is in charge of the champagne and the icy tubs of oysters, and to look for Stevie, her nine-year-old son. Stevie is where she knows he will be—watching the party from the edge, slouched, meditatively chewing his hand. The white tuxedo he picked out himself, at the antique store where Christine bought her thirties lawn dress, hangs on him like a zoot suit.

Many of the wedding guests wear elegant vintage clothes, or costly new ones designed to look vintage: peplums, organza, cabbage roses, white suits, and Panama hats; it is late afternoon, mid-July and unseasonably hot, so that quite a few of the guests look, like the garden, bleached of color and slightly blown. For a moment Christine wishes they'd held the wedding in June, when the irises and the peonies were in bloom; then she remembers it wasn't till May that they made up their minds to get married.

At first she tries to vary the dog-bite story from telling to telling—to keep herself interested, and for John's sake; John has had to listen to this thirty times. But finally she gives up. She says: "I stopped at a barn sale near Lenox. I was crossing the road. A big black dog, some kind of shepherd-Labrador mix, came charging out of nowhere and sunk its teeth in my leg. I screamed—I think I screamed. A woman came out of a barn and called the dog. It backed off right away."

Even as she tells it, Christine knows: despite its suddenness, its randomness, the actually getting bitten, it isn't much of a story. It lacks what a good dog story needs, that extra dimension of the undoglike and bizarre. She and John used to have a terrific dog story about their collie, Alexander—a story they told happily for a few years, then got bored with and told reluctantly when party talk turned to dog stories. At some point they had agreed that telling dog stories marked a real conversational low, and from then on they were self-conscious, embarrassed to tell theirs. That was even before Alexander died.

Yet today, as they greet their guests and the talk drifts from Christine's bite to dogs in general, Christine realizes that she now has another dog story. She tells it, she cannot avoid it, and the guests respond with escalating dog stories: dumb dogs, tricky dogs, lucky dogs with windfall inheritances, mean dogs that bite. From time to time John or Christine senses that the other is on the verge of telling the story about Alexander. Although they are both quite willing to hear it, both are relieved when the other holds back. Christine feels that this—thinking of the story and knowing the other is also thinking of it and not telling it—connects them more strongly than the ceremony about to take place.

Perhaps her dog-bite story would be livelier if she added some of the details that, for laziness and other private reasons, she has decided to leave out. She can't talk about the woman, the dog's owner, without hearing an edge of shrill complaint and nasty gossip about how awful strangers can be; your own wedding seems like a peculiar place to be sounding like that.

When the woman got hold of the dog, she had stayed a few feet away, not moving. The dog got quiet instantly.

The woman said, "You scared of dogs?"

Christine's leg didn't really hurt yet, but her heart was pounding. "We used to have a dog," she said.

The woman cut her off. "They always know when you're scared," she said. Only then did she drag the dog away. "Don't move," she told Christine.

She came back with a bottle of alcohol. It could have been kerosene, yet Christine let her splash it on her leg. The pain made Christine's knees go rubbery. She turned and weaved toward the car. Probably the woman was right to yell after her, "Hey, you shouldn't drive!"

Nearly all the wedding guests know that Christine is pregnant; it's part of the sympathy her dog-bite story evokes, and why everyone winces when she tells it. Men tend to ask about the dog: What's being done, has it bitten anyone before? The women ask about Stevie. Everyone is relieved to hear that Stevie was home with John. It isn't just his having been spared the sight of his mother being hurt, but that most of the guests have seen Stevie around dogs—any dog except Alexander. He simply turns to stone. It has taken Christine years not to smile apologetically as she pulls Stevie off to the car.

All week the house has been full of visiting friends, teenagers hired to help out, carpenters converting part of the barn into a studio for Christine. It is her wedding present from John, for which she feels so grateful that she refrains from mentioning that the construction should have been finished weeks ago. And no wonder. All but one of the carpenters were on a perpetual coffee break at her kitchen table, smoking Camels and flirting with the catering girls, though the one the girls liked was the handsome one, Robert, who was never at the table but out working in the barn.

Christine began taking refuge in the studio, watching Robert work. A few days ago, she invited Robert to the wedding. Now she looks for him and sees him standing not far from Stevie.

Putting her weight on her good leg, Christine leans against John. "Sit down," he says. "Take it easy." He has been saying this since she got pregnant, more often since the bite. But if she greets the guests sitting, she will just have to talk about that. She tells herself that none of it —the adrenaline, the tetanus shot, the pain—has in fact been harmful. She wants desperately to protect the baby, though in the beginning she argued against having it. John said he understood, but she had to realize: Stevie was a baby for so long. It won't be like that again.

No one here has met Stevie's dad, who went back to Philadelphia when Stevie was fifteen months old. One thing Christine likes about being settled is that she got tired of explaining. Describing how Stevie's dad left right after learning that something was really wrong with Stevie, she was often uncertain how angry or self-righteous or sympathetic to sound.

When Stevie was two she had moved here to the country, found a rented house and a woman to watch him while she supported them, substitute-teaching art. Evenings, she would have long, loud conversations from across the house with Stevie, who couldn't yet sit up. That was when she met John. John has a small construction company; he built the house they live in. When Christine and Stevie moved in, she quit teaching, put Stevie in a special day program in Pittsfield, and was able to paint full time. Stevie loves John, and signs of Christine and John's success are everywhere: the house, the garden, the nail-polish-red Ferrari that Annette, Christine's art dealer, has just this moment driven up from New York.

Annette wears white pedal pushers and an enormous white man's shirt; her leopard high heels sink into the lawn so that pulling them out gives her walk a funny bounce. She plows through a circle surrounding Christine and John, first hugs, then briskly shakes hands with them both, then looks down at Christine's bandage and says, "I hope they crucified Rin Tin Tin." Christine wonders how literally Annette means this; she remembers a recent art piece, some sort of ecological statement involving a crucified stuffed coyote.

"The dog's under observation," says Christine. "The doctor called the town sheriff—"

"Observation!" Annette says. "At the end of a loaded gun. Well, I don't know. Why would anyone want a dog? Remember when Wegman's dog got lost and he put up signs on the lampposts and of course the signs got recognized and taken down—they're worth fortunes now."

"Did he ever find the dog?" John asks.

"Of course not," says Annette.

"That's fabulous," says John. Christine has often noticed how quickly Annette makes people sound like her, use her words—even John, who likes Annette, but not for the reasons Annette thinks. He isn't fooled by her asking him for business advice; he knows she has a perfectly good, high-powered accountant of her own.

Annette wedges herself between John and Christine, leans toward Christine, and says, "Let's see the new studio."

But John and Christine are watching a tall man with Donahue-platinum hair bounding toward them across the lawn. It's the minister, Hal Koch. "Like in the cola," he said when they went to see him in his study; Christine thought he must say that often, a good man guiding strangers in their choice between a soda and a dirty word.

She'd wanted to go to a justice of the peace, elope without leaving town. But John wants something more formal, guests and God as witnesses that now she is really his. John has a religious streak, inherited no doubt from his mother, a wraith-like woman in an orange dress and wooden yoga beads, now edging timidly toward Stevie.

Without even registering Annette, Hal Koch shakes hands with John, then Christine. He says, "Terrific place!" Within a few seconds he is questioning John about construction costs. John answers patiently, though Christine can tell it is driving him mad; it is a measure of his sweetness and patience that he will not even let himself catch her eye. In fact, she likes it that this sort of talk can take place, that people know John, respect him, know what to say. Christine had been grateful for this in Hal Koch's study, because John and the minister kept quietly talking about John's business while Stevie was switching the overhead light on and off as fast as he could.

When Stevie finally stopped, Hal had said, "He's a beautiful kid."

"I've learned a lot from him," John said. "I feel like I'm privileged to know him."

This is how John stands up for Stevie, by telling the truth: there is more to Stevie than anyone suspects. But there is also the way John says "know him" and a funny thing he does with his eyes; she has seen him do it so many times and never has figured out how exactly he tells people without a word that Stevie isn't his. Everyone seems to catch on, even Hal Koch, who redirected his compliment to Christine. It isn't that John is disowning Stevie, distancing himself beyond ill luck or faulty genes. He just wants extra credit. And really, he deserves it. People who admire John for taking on Stevie can't imagine what it's meant. It's partly why this wedding—why John and Christine's life—makes the guests feel so good that a little dog bite can't touch it.

John and Christine and the minister walk over to the rose arbor. Everyone gathers round. The guests have nearly fallen silent when John holds up his hand and walks over and gets Stevie and pulls him under the arbor with them. He leans Stevie back against his stomach and joins his arms in a V down Stevie's chest. Stevie looks pleased. A wave of emotion rises up from the guests, a tide of pleasure and sympathy. And suddenly Christine hates them. It's not that she doesn't value their kindness but that she will scream if one more person, however genuinely, wishes her well.

Of course her nerves are raw: three months pregnant, the heat, the nonstop achy drumbeat of blood in her leg—and on top of that, getting married. She is glad that the service is short, the bare-bones civil ceremony, glad that it all goes by very fast and in a kind of fog. In his study, Hal Koch had asked if they wanted a prayer or a poem—he said lots of couples chose poems. He put this question to Christine, though the wedding was John's idea. Christine said, "How about the Twenty-third Psalm?" and there had been a funny moment when the two men fell silent and looked at her until she laughed and said, "Joke."

With evening, the perfumy scent of the tall white lilies fills the entire garden. This is the worst time of year. It used to be taken for granted that people go crazy around midsummer night and stay up all night in the grip of unruly dreams and desires. All day the sun gives the world a hallucinatory buckle, and even in the evening, after a shower, heat seems to keep shimmering behind your eyes like the ocean's roll after a voyage. No one could look at the trees and the flowers and not know that this is their peak.

The air is humid and sweet, and the green of the grass is the brightest it has been all day. Christine feels suddenly dizzy. She's sure she can get away with a glass of white wine, but a few of the guests seem less certain, and before they move on to the lemon tarragon chicken and spinach salad, their glances stray accusingly toward her glass. John helps Stevie fill his plate. Christine sees Robert walking across the lawn toward the studio. There is something she wants to tell him: the reason she'd stopped at that barn sale was that they were selling a work sink she knew would be perfect for the studio. Maybe if the sink is still there, Robert could drive by and look at it.

Inside the studio, Robert leans against a sawhorse, slowly smoking a joint. He holds it out to Christine, and though she knows it is madness getting stoned at your wedding, with all its social obligations, and probably terrible for the baby, she takes it, takes a drag. Soon she feels uncomfortable standing, looks around for something to lean on, and nearly backs into the table saw before Robert points and yells, "Yo!"

"That's all I need," says Christine. "A little something to match the dog tooth marks in my leg."

"It's strange about weddings," says Robert. "I've noticed. People tend to get seriously accident-prone. One of my brothers got married with his arm in a sling, and a cousin got married in a neck brace."

"At the same time?" asks Christine. "What happened?"

"Different times." Robert laughs. "I don't know. My brother was hunting, fell out of a tree. The cousin I think was in a car wreck. How's your leg?"

"Fine," Christine says, and then for some reason says, "Really? Really, it hurts."

Robert says, "I'll take a look at it for you." His voice has in it an unmistakable flirty edge, and Christine is pleasantly shocked, not so much by the sexual suggestion—which he can only make because he is younger and working for her and this is her wedding day and nothing can possibly come of it—as by the intimacy of his daring to joke about so serious a subject as her dog bite. In some ways it presumes more, makes some bolder claim than John's unfailing solicitousness, and, by distracting her, works better to reassure her and dull the pain. She fears that Robert will ask what happened exactly and that she'll get halfway through the story and stop. But what he says is, "Was that the barn sale out on 7, a couple houses past the Carvel?"

"That's the one," Christine says.

"I stopped there," says Robert. "Believe it or not. They were selling a work sink—big slabs of bluestone, copper fixtures, enormous, you could see it from the road. It will be great for this place. It was only a hundred and twenty-five bucks. If you guys don't want to pay for it, we can call it a wedding present from me. This must have been after you were there. There was no sign of a dog. I'm going back with some friends this week to help load it onto the pickup . . ."

Robert rattles on, clearly worried about spending John's money, and so doesn't see Christine's eyes fill with tears. One thing she'd thought as she stopped at the sale was how good the sink would look in the studio, and the other—she knew this and blamed herself at the moment the dog ran toward her and even thought this was *why* she was getting bitten—was the pleasure of telling Robert she'd found it; they had been talking a lot about sinks. This is another part of the story she's told no one. She feels as if she has been caught in some dreadful O. Henry plot, some "Gift of the Magi" sort of thing, except that couple were newlyweds and in it together and on their way up. The implications of this happening to her and Robert are in every way less simple.

All week, she has been saying that she fears the finishing of the studio because it means she must start working again. But that, she realizes now, isn't the reason at all. She feels as if just telling Robert that she, too, stopped for the sink would add up to more than it is, to some sort of declaration, an irrevocable act—though most likely he would just see it as your ordinary, everyday believe-it-or-not.

"Thank you," she says. Even this comes out more heartfelt than she'd planned. She is so uncertain of what to say next that she's almost relieved when Annette walks in.

"What a space!" Annette says. "God, I could fit my whole loft in that corner."

"Robert built most of it," Christine says and is instantly sorry. Annette wheels on Robert with that fleeting but intense curiosity—part affected, part sincere—that art-world people seem to have for anyone who actually does anything. As Annette looks at Robert, Christine wishes she'd given her the lightning studio tour, once around and out the door—she might not have even *seen* him. But isn't this what Christine wants, some version of the appreciation she desires when Annette comes to look at her work?

Robert looks directly at Annette and smiles. Annette gives him her three-second downtown grin, but so good-humoredly and with such invitation that a wave of jealousy, loneliness, and embarrassment overcomes Christine. Why should she feel that way now? She, after all, is the bride. Her being the bride is probably why Robert sees no disloyalty in turning so easily from her to Annette.

"How *are* you?" Annette asks Christine, meaning—it's clear from her tone—the pregnancy, not the bite. She's trying hard to focus, to not let her sudden interest in Robert make her exclude Christine. But she is only making things worse, making Christine feel damaged, out of the running, like some guy with a war wound in a Hemingway novel.

"All right," Christine says. "The dog bite didn't help."

"God," Annette says. "I just remembered. That's what happened to Jo-Jo the Dog Boy's mother. She got bitten by a dog when she was pregnant. Remember Jo-Jo the Dog Boy?"

"I sure do," Robert says. "Poor guy. The real-life Chewy-Chewbacca." Both he and Annette seem pleased to have found this bit of trivia knowledge in common.

"Great," says Christine. "Thanks a lot. That's just what I need to hear."

"Chris*tine*," says Annette. "No one believes that stuff anymore."

"What are we talking about?" Robert says. The fact of Christine's pregnancy seems to have just dawned on him. "Double congratulations!" he says. "I wondered why you guys would bother getting married after all this time."

He can't resist looking at Christine's belly. That he feels free to do this—and that he hadn't known, though she'd assumed that everyone knew—reminds Christine of what it's like to be pregnant: a secret for so long, and, even when it is obvious, still a secret—all those secret shifts and movements no one else can feel. When she was pregnant with Stevie, that summer in New York, she used to walk down the street and feel herself skimming over the pavement, encased with Stevie in a bubble, one of those membraned, gelatinous eggs out of Hieronymus Bosch. That is how she feels now, that this bubble containing her and the child is hovering slightly above the studio floor, rising toward the window, then floating down again, near enough to see Robert and Annette moving closer by millimeters. Suddenly she is stung with envy, though not of Robert and Annette or their lives—which, she tells herself, lack everything she treasures most about her own life. She feels that her life is closing down; it has always been closed down.

It takes a while for the audio to come back. When it does, Annette is saying, "People say dogs are smart. It's something people say. People who never had dogs. I say, compared to what? Cats? In my experience dogs are very, very dumb. When I was growing up in Anchorage, the family across from us had a dog team they'd let pull the kids down the hill in front of their house, and one day the dogs pulled the sled and three kids right in the path of a snowplow. Brilliant."

"Jesus," Robert says. And a moment later, "You grew up in Anchorage?"

"Some dogs are smart," says Christine. "Alexander."

"Well," says Annette. "Alexander. Christine's dog."

"What kind of dog was he?" Robert asks.

"A romantic," Annette says.

Robert looks quizzically at Christine. And now there is no way for Christine not to say it, not to tell the story she has been thinking about all day: "Alexander fell in love. With a female collie down in Sheffield. He met her when we left him there with friends, one weekend we went away. The female lived up the road from our friends. She was in heat when we picked Alexander up, so we took her home with us, but she kept running away. So we brought her back to Sheffield, and the next day Alexander disappeared. He'd never run away before. We

thought he was dead. And two days later our friends called
to say he'd shown up at the collie family's house."

"Sheffield's fifteen miles away," Robert says.

"Fourteen point five," Christine says. "We clocked it."
She remembers watching the odometer on John's pickup,
proud of their dog and jubilant that he was not only alive
but in love. How eager they had been to fuse their lives
then, for Stevie to be John's child, Alexander to be Christine's dog. But Alexander was never really—as Annette
just called him—Christine's dog. She still misses him,
but it is John who took him to the vet when she was
down in the city, John who, without ever saying much,
has grieved.

She remembers the night they went to get Alexander
from the collie family: the family lived in a tiny house,
a cabin, the dogs were inside, stuck together, everyone
was laughing, jumping out of their way, it was impossible
to talk, but even so it seemed wrong to separate them.
They left Alexander there until the female went out of
heat and he was ready to come home.

Robert and Annette are waiting for more, but Christine
has nothing to say. She is sorry she told the story. She
thinks she has told it at the wrong time, to the wrong
people, for entirely the wrong reasons, and for a moment
it seems likely that she will never tell it again. And what
good can come from telling a story about a dog that was
more capable of passion than its owners may ever be?
She gives Annette and Robert a little wave. Then she
goes outside.

The light is almost gone. The guests have finished their

food and are sitting at the tables, talking quietly. On each table is a lighted candle inside a paper bag. The muted lights are at once festive and unbearably sad. Christine looks around for Stevie, whom—after a scary minute or two—she spots in the field behind the house. She had been searching for the white suit, but Stevie has changed his outfit. He has borrowed someone's black silk jacket with a map of Guam on the back; it comes nearly down to his knees. On his head is a set of stereo headphones, and instead of shoes he wears his winter moon-boots, silver Mylar that catches the light, thick soles that raise him inches off the ground. He is stalking fireflies in the high grass, lifting his legs very high, like a deer.

Christine is watching so intently that she jumps when John comes up beside her. They stand in easy silence for a few moments and then John says, "It doesn't feel different, does it? Being married? It feels exactly the same."

At first Christine doesn't answer, but keeps on watching Stevie, who is moving his head oddly, again like a deer, as if he is tracking fireflies, not by looking for light, but by listening. Several doctors told them that Stevie is partly deaf. Each time, Christine and John sat in the office, nodding, thinking about the fact that often, when they were home alone with Stevie, he would stand and go to the door, minutes before it was possible to hear John's truck or Christine's car in the driveway. John used to say it was something Stevie had picked up from Alexander.

John's face, in silhouette, strains forward. Staring across the dark lawn, he is trying very deliberately not to seem as if he is waiting for her to reply.

"It's fine," Christine tells him. "Nothing's changed. We've always been married," she says.

IMAGINARY

PROBLEMS

DOUG (my wife calls her therapist Doug) says our family needs a mourning ritual, a formal rite to bring us together over what has been lost and what's left. Doug's office is full of primitive masks. I focused on a cone of ropy hair as he told us about the Amazonian tribe which, when too much went wrong, sent someone out to kill a jaguar and bury it under the headman's house. I said, "We can do in the hamster."

"Hamster?" said Doug.

"Murph," said Beth. "Buzzy's hamster." Doug looked reproachful, as if his not knowing about the hamster made him wonder what else she'd withheld.

Not long after, the hamster died of natural causes. I felt it was my fault.

If you were driving beside us, stalled at the entrance to the West Side Highway, it would never occur to you that in our trunk is a half-frozen hamster we are on our way to bury on my sister's farm. When you saw our quiet children, our twelve-year-old daughter, Holly, our six-year-old son, Buzzy, you would think they are better than your kids and wonder how we do it. How could you know that the children's silence scares us, though Beth—in that quiet voice, in which, from their infancy, she half pretended they couldn't hear—says, "Aren't the kids being great? They always come through when we need them." This is no more true than that the kids can't hear. Sometimes they come through, sometimes they don't. I have always been amazed by the places they could fight: crowded waiting rooms, the back seats of cars on icy drives. Now what we need from them is to fight as if nothing had happened, to bicker and scream like before.

So much has gone wrong, it seems gratuitous of Doug to trace it back so far: he says our problems began when I went alone to Jacksonville after my stepmother's death—that I was angry at Beth and the kids for not coming with me. I don't remember that. I remember it rained at La Guardia and later in Florida, too. Rain swept over the fuselage. I stayed in my seat in the warm bright plane, not wanting to ever get off—not stuck there, exactly, nothing like that, but just for the moment happy.

The road from the Jacksonville airport was half under water, and as the cab slowed down to part the oily floods, the driver said, "There's a funny thing about this town. Sometimes on summer nights when it rains, you see puddles on the city streets—hopping, hopping with frogs."

"Frogs?" I said. "From where?"

"The ocean," he said. "I don't know."

As my father and I drove through the rain to Paglio's Pizza, I mentioned this. He said frogs didn't hatch out of puddles. Already he'd found a restaurant where all the waitresses knew him. There was no real food in his house. My stepmother had cooked natural food; the kitchen was full of grains and rice, jars of apricots and cashews. She had many health theories, like seasonal migration to alternate wet climates with dry. The accident had happened on a dude ranch near Tucson. They had just gotten back from a hike. She took a sip of soda from a can into which a wasp had fallen; it stung her on the tongue, and ten minutes later she was dead.

I asked why the ranch didn't have a bee-sting kit. My father and I are both lawyers; we both knew he could have recovered the cost of a mini-ranch of his own. We didn't talk about that. The phone rang often. I knocked around the house. All day I put off calling Beth and the kids; once I did it, I couldn't look forward to it anymore. But when at last I talked to Beth, I was flipping through the Jacksonville phone book. The kids spoke too low or too fast, I couldn't hear, couldn't follow, couldn't imagine their faces. I couldn't wait to get off the phone.

The children know too much. That, too, is Doug's idea. He says we put Band-Aids on wounds that would heal faster in the air. It's strange, making Band-Aids sound so primitive and in the next breath praising people who bury jaguars under the headman's house. I remember Band-Aids with love—the little red string that opens the wrappers, the rubber-adhesive smell.

Somewhere the Palisades turn into the Thruway. I have lost track of time. Six weeks, two months ago, I sat in guilty silence while Beth told the children their father had fallen in love with someone else, but now he was home, that was over. The good news was that Beth was pregnant, they were going to have a baby brother or sister. Beth had cooked pasta and lemon veal. I'd thrown some asparagus on. I should have pared the asparagus bottoms. Holly peeled back the hard asparagus skin, curling it in strips. Buzzy said, "Hey, that's cool," and I thought he meant the baby. But he meant what Holly was doing, and then he did it, too. I said, "Don't play with your food."

Buzzy said, "We don't need another kid," as if we should all just change our minds and return it like the flannel sleepers Beth's parents still sometimes sent.

Two weeks later, Beth called me at work. I ran out and got a cab. Beth was waiting under the hospital awning. Her face was geisha-white. I couldn't believe the emergency room had just let her leave on her own. A lawsuit flashed through my mind and flashed out again. I thought of the ranch without the first aid to save my stepmother's life.

Beth slumped in the back of the cab. When we got home she went to bed. She said, "Martin, you tell the kids." The kids didn't seem to care about the baby; they were worried about Beth. I reassured them, thinking how much time had passed. I couldn't remember telling them how babies were born. Now clearly they knew how they weren't. Beth got her strength back soon, but she couldn't get over the miscarriage—she was just streaming grief. It was right after this that she got me to go to Doug's office, and Doug told us we needed a ritual.

We are not the same people we were. A year before, if I'd volunteered the hamster for ritual purposes, Beth would have burst out laughing. A year before, we would never have been in Doug's office, with its good rugs and well-lit niches housing statuettes of pre-Columbian birth goddesses. But so much had gone wrong, so much changed and unpredictably lost, everything felt up for grabs, ready and waiting for another wasp swimming furiously in its pitch-black Pepsi sea.

On the morning Buzzy ran into the living room and said Murph wasn't moving, Beth and I exchanged looks. It was the first time in months we'd looked at each other like that—a look that was like speech.

I said, "Isn't that strange? Remember, in Doug's office? You think Murph could have died for our sins?"

"Your sins," said Beth, and then, miraculously, laughed. We went into Buzzy's room. Beth said, "We can't just throw him out."

I said, "Okay, let's bury him under the headman's house."

"We should bury him *somewhere*," said Beth. "It's what families always did. We buried our goldfish in the back yard. Didn't you?"

I said, "My family didn't have a back yard. Nor, do I have to point out, do we."

Beth thought a minute. Then she said, "If you can believe you killed Murph by mentioning him in Doug's office, I can believe it would help us to bury him in the ground."

I told her I hadn't been serious about putting a jinx on Murph. Should I have tried harder to convince her? For a lawyer, I am surprisingly unlitigious. I am retained by a mega-construction firm that tears down large buildings and puts up larger ones; I am not paid to argue in court but to see that we never get there.

I said, "What we have here is city life. Where to bury the family pet?"

No one could see digging a grave in Central Park or some patch of Westchester woods. We thought of my sister's farm. I called Peg, who said come up, she'd love to see us, but her house was full of people two weekends in a row. I couldn't say it was urgent.

When Buzzy realized that Murph was really dead, he sat on his bed and wailed. We had the hamster in a shoe box on the fire escape. The weather was getting warmer. Beth said, "Let's put it in the freezer."

Beth told the children that night, gave them—as Doug suggested—a fully worked-out plan. In three weeks, we would go up to Peg's and bury Murph. The children said, "Fine." That they didn't seem to think it was strange was fairly strange in itself; they both have that overdeveloped child's sense of what is and isn't disgusting. Well, despite everything, we're their parents; you can't blame them for looking to us for guidance on what to do with the dead.

By then it was hard to feel Murph's loss. Not that I'd felt his presence much—he was mostly Buzzy and Beth's. Still, any death was a death, an absence in the house. Despite what Doug thinks, I am not afraid of sadness— quite the contrary, I'd say. But once we had Murph in the freezer, loss became a joke, a sign of confusion and distance and change which I avoid with random thoughts of work or food or pure survival as I fight for a lane in the press toward the Bear Mountain exit.

Imaginary Problems

Doug has told Beth that I did what I did because I had never grieved over my mother; my stepmother's death brought it back. He said I was out of touch with my feelings. He sent us an article, from a women's magazine, about a guy who was eating dinner one night and started hemorrhaging from the throat. Three operations, a repaired major blood vessel, and two years of therapy later, he realized that all his emotions had been locked there, in his throat. Now he expresses them more. When I read that, I thought: He was already expressing them in his own way. Am I wrong in thinking that a family has a language of its own, that I did not have to bleed all over the lemon veal and the tough asparagus, that everything was clear enough from the tone in which I told my children to stop playing with their food?

When I was a child there were toy steering wheels that attached to the back of the front seat. I wore out a dozen of them, oversteering wildly as my father drove and my sister lay flat on the ledge behind the seat and looked out the back window. This was before seat belts and child safety. For years before I could drive, I dreamed about driving as flight, as freedom, a way of being with girls, the car as an extension of my body. Beth used to have panic dreams in which she was driving before she knew how; I never had dreams like that. Doug doesn't approve of cars. He says they are bubbles that keep us apart, each in our separate world. He thinks we were better off walking single file through the jungle. I have never been in the jungle, and neither, as far as I know, has Doug.

No one has spoken for thirty miles when Beth says, "Doug's thinking of giving up his practice and going to graduate school in anthropology."

I say, "He'll quit when he can't find a tribe to pay him a hundred an hour."

Doug was a mistake. It wasn't a time when any of us was thinking clearly. Beth knew something was wrong but not what, and I couldn't tell her. I asked a malpractice lawyer I knew. I said: Someone professional, not a crackpot, someone who won't convince her she's hated me all along. By accident, my friend and one of Beth's friends both gave us Doug's name; we mistook coincidence for consensus. I expected an elderly Viennese, not some guy with stringy hair and a necklace made of teeth.

Beth used to be funnier, used to talk more. Her hands flew around when she spoke. Now I reach out to touch Beth's hand, though that is no longer simple. When we met, I had an old Pontiac I drove with Beth practically in my lap. Now we have bucket seats. Couples who'd laugh at single beds have no problem with this. Beth doesn't see me reach for her hand, which is tucked in a corner of the armrest, so my groping for it has all the grace of wrestling a jacket off while you're driving.

We are sharp, realistic people. We have senses of humor, I think. Then how to explain why we're here, believing or at least pretending that the pain of loss, of adultery and miscarriage, can be eased by mumbling some mumbo-jumbo and committing to earth a frozen rodent in an extra-large Ziploc bag?

One morning last summer, a guy in my office said, "Guess who's coming to the Ninth Avenue site."

"Madonna," I said. I'd been corresponding with some people trying to pitch a rock video to Madonna—a video filmed at our site with lots of guys walking high steel.

"Better," he said. "Cookie the Clown."

"*The* Cookie?" I said.

My supervisor was embarrassed when he told me I had to be there. He said, "If, God forbid, Cookie gets flattened, I need someone around I can count on. Come on, Martin. You'll be a hero to your kids."

A hero to my kids: Holly knew very well who Cookie was but pretended not to. Buzzy had only recently switched from clowns to baseball cards, but he hit his forehead with his palm and took an elaborate pratfall and shouted up from the ground: "Cookie the Clown? That's sick!"

This wasn't so long after my stepmother's death. I remember thinking that the steady drizzle falling on Cookie's set was the same rain that fell on Jacksonville. That day I saw it as Cookie's set, although it was our building.

The site was covered with puddles and mud. It wasn't raining too hard for the video crew to shoot, just hard enough to drench them. Cookie put on a slicker and explained to the boys and girls that work goes on in all weather. I was riveted, not by my job or the sight of

Cookie in a bulldozer, but because I was standing next to a woman I desperately wanted to talk to. Her name was Marian. She was some kind of troubleshooter from the show; she was the one who helped Cookie into his slicker. We'd said hello and discussed the rain, but I wanted to say something else. I kept looking up at the sky, rolling my eyes and shrugging.

I hung around till she'd packed everyone into the vans. By then we were totally soaked. We went to a hamburger joint. She asked about my job. I asked her what it was like working for Cookie the Clown. She said you had to be careful. It wouldn't look good for Cookie to sue or be sued.

I said, "There was one year when Holly was small, I don't think Buzzy was born yet; my wife used to say the two people she hated most in the world were Richard Nixon and Cookie the Clown." Marian laughed, but I got flustered, quoting Beth, bringing in the kids. I felt I had ruined everything.

And that, more or less, was that. We said goodbye, we shook hands. But I couldn't get her off my mind. I would walk down the street, staring at strangers' faces, wondering how many perfectly normal people were right at that moment obsessed with someone they hardly knew and had chosen almost at random to fix on with what, for want of a better word, you might as well call love. I felt like John Hinckley. I thought: It would be easier to shoot the President than to call her. But finally I called. We met for lunch. She said that my calling had made her so happy she was sure she'd be run over by a car on the way to meet me.

I couldn't tell Beth. Of course she knew something was wrong. I knew she was suffering, but couldn't explain—that was the hardest part. I kept asking, Is it me? In fact, I had never been so present. I had time and patience for everything—unraveling the children's shoe-laces, settling their fights. I actually *talked* to the children, though I can't now recall about what.

One day I persuaded Buzzy to watch Cookie the Clown with me. He had, as I said, outgrown it. But he was so surprised I asked, he agreed at once. Cookie was tour-ing an underground mushroom mine. The millions of fat white mushrooms waiting to be picked were a lovely sight, though not, I imagine, to the women who worked there, day after day in the dark. One of the workers told Cookie that each mushroom was different, like snow-flakes. "Like people," Cookie said, and she said, "Very much like people." "Buzzy," I said, "mushrooms are *nothing* like people."

Beth said her problems had nothing to do with me. She felt that her sense of the world had gone sour—curdled, she said, like milk. She woke me in the middle of the night to talk—in a hot, dry, panicky voice. Some guy on the street had looked at her a second too long and she'd thought he was going to kill her. She began to hate going out. I said, Talk to someone. Someone who isn't me.

I have to admit I was grateful at first, glad even for

Doug's dental jewelry and Guatemalan poncho. I thought: They'll talk more about jaguar rites, less about me. Even when it struck me that my wife was telling him secrets she didn't tell me, I thought: Well, I deserve it.

Maybe I will never know why Beth decided to get pregnant. At the time I didn't ask; now I no longer can. I am sure it was a choice—we had been married fourteen years; both Holly and Buzzy were planned. For all I know, it was Doug's idea. Maybe Beth thought it would fix things, restore what had gone bad, like those cookbook tricks for fixing the spoiled hollandaise, the overthickened gravy.

And it did, it worked. As soon as Beth told me—as soon as it really sank in—images began streaming through my mind, pictures from our lives. One image stayed with me: when Buzzy was tiny, someone gave us a beanbag chair. Beth used to scoop him out a little hollow in the chair, and the two of them would lie there watching MTV. She'd said the videos were the perfect length for her and Buzzy's attention span. It's always the most trivial things that call us back to ourselves—never what you might expect. When I thought of that—Beth and Buzzy watching MTV—everything that had happened since seemed to dissolve, and I understood that my life with Beth and the children was my real life, and everything else was a dream.

That same night, I told Beth about Marian. I promised it was over. I called Marian and met her for lunch and told her Beth was pregnant—that was the reason I gave. At first Marian couldn't see what difference it made; I couldn't really explain. Finally she smiled and said she'd learned her lesson from me. From now on, she was sticking to guys in clown noses and size-15 checkered shoes. That was my moment of sharpest regret; because, even then, we could still joke around. At home, nothing was funny.

That wasn't completely true. For that short time Beth was pregnant, something lightened; we could laugh about getting it right this time, or getting a child with all Buzzy's and Holly's worst faults. Then came the miscarriage. After that, we sat in Doug's office. I joked about Murph. I was the only one laughing.

When the traffic lets up, I say into my rearview mirror, "Nancy and Ronald Reagan go into a restaurant. Nancy says, 'I'll have the meat and potatoes.' 'And for the vegetable?' says the waiter. And Nancy says, 'He'll have the meat and potatoes, too.' "

Beth says, "Martin, that's awful." Buzzy bursts out laughing. Holly says, "Why are *you* laughing? I bet you don't even get it."

"Vegetable?" I say. "Ronald Reagan?"

"*I* get it," says Holly. "I think it's really mean."

"Toward Reagan?" I say. "Or toward vegetables in general?"

"I don't know," Holly says. "Toward both." Holly flips back and forth about us, always so as to find fault. Sometimes I'm too soft and sometimes I lack compassion. Sometimes we're too rich and sometimes too poor. Once, in fifth grade, Holly had to bring into school an anecdote from her very early childhood. It was a terrible moment: I couldn't remember one. Beth came up with something for her, but Holly stayed angry at me. I remember telling her that it wasn't a question of love or attention, but strictly a memory problem.

Doug says the whole point of ritual is remembering. He says they fix things in time, in the mind; they work like primitive record-keeping, tying knots in string. He says, "Time is the string, rituals the knots." That doesn't sound right to me. Anything worth its own ritual, you would remember without one. You'd know why you buried that jaguar under the headman's house.

Two exits from my sister's, I ask Beth how we should work this. Get out of the car and start digging a hole? Or wait, let Murph defrost? Sneak off on the sly? Invite everyone? Beth looks at me and blinks. The morning sun is harsh. She says, "Let's play it by ear."

In the uproar of arrival, Murph is forgotten. Buzzy jumps out and races in circles around the car with his cousin Jed. Holly heads across the field to toss sticks for Peg's dogs. My sister runs out and wraps her arms around me and squeezes. It's been so long since anyone hugged me that way, I decide to tell Peg everything, to get her alone and confess.

Eugene, Peg's husband, shakes my hand. His handshake matches the rest of him—bony and a bit stiff.

Eugene is a semi-famous painter with a reputation built on perfect hard-edge stripes. At least he and Beth can talk about paint. Once during each visit Eugene says you couldn't pay him to live in Manhattan now, he gets so sick of hearing everyone talk real estate. After that, it is impossible for me to mention my work.

When Eugene's paintings are selling, he drinks Mexican beer. When they aren't, it's Genesee. Everyone knows this, and, insofar as you can kid Eugene, we kid him about it. Now Beth and I get our choice of Tecate or Sol. We drink a couple of beers, then Eugene asks Beth to come see his studio. Before I can steer the conversation toward what's on my mind, Peg says, "I need to talk to you about Dad." She's seen him more recently than I, three weeks ago; on the phone, she'd said he was fine.

Now she says, "Not *exactly* fine. I guess he's okay. But listen. I went into the bathroom, and when I closed the door this *thing* jumped at me from the back of the door, her dressing gown, silk, good lace, very Miss Havisham. It swung out from its hook, puffed a puff of lavender, then swung back."

I wonder why she's telling me this. "You think it was her ghost?"

"Ghost?" says Peg. "I think it was her dressing gown. It's been a year since she died."

"Maybe he's wearing it," I say, and we both start to laugh.

"That's disgusting," says Peg.

We fall silent, drinking our beer. Peg says, "You spend your life eating whole grains and nuts and you come back from a hike, take your first sip of Pepsi in thirty years, and bingo, good night, you're dead." There is an edge in her voice.

I say, "How are things going?" I hold up my Tecate can. "Looks like they're going okay."

"Terrible," she says. "Eugene is seeing someone. The thing is, it happened before, with this same woman. Two years ago."

"Really?" I'm horrified by how hopeful this makes me feel.

"Really," she says, and I understand I can't tell her. Eugene and I should be talking, Beth commiserating with Peg. Peg says, "How are things with you?"

"Fine," I say, and Peg says, "Sure. Beth looks completely zombified."

"Oh," I say, "you noticed. Well, the miscarriage . . ."

Beth and Eugene walk in. After an uneasy silence, Beth says, "It's wonderful. Eugene's doing something totally new." I think, That's not what I hear. But Eugene isn't thinking that. When you talk to Eugene about his work, there are no double entendres, no subtexts.

Beth catches my eye and says, "We should get some stuff out of the car." I know she means Murph.

Beth turns to Peg and Eugene. "I hope this doesn't sound crazy to you," she says, "but Murph, Buzzy's hamster, died, we needed somewhere to bury it, we brought it . . ."

Eugene looks pleased; the spectacle of city dwellers with nowhere to bury their dead confirms him. I search his face, but there is nothing for me there, no fellow-sinner recognition.

Peg says, "It's not crazy at all. Just bury it deep. Remember, Martin, we had that turtle that died and we just covered it with dirt, and the cat dug it up in the middle of the night and smeared turtle guts all over Mom's kitchen?"

"Where was I?" I ask.

Eugene says, "Let me get you a shovel." Beth and I go to the car. The children are playing in the field. I open the trunk. Murph is in an opaque white plastic shopping bag; his Baggie is inside that.

Beth says, "Would you hold Murph a second?" She reaches into the trunk, gets another white plastic bag, and takes out a small container of strawberry yogurt.

"What's that?" I say. "Food for the dead? An afterlife snack for Murph?"

"It's the baby," she says. "The fetus. I saved it. I thought I was being crazy, but I discussed it with Doug. And he said I was right. I think we should bury it. Near Murph."

"You *were* being crazy," I said. "You are. You've gone totally around the bend. You've got a fetus in there? Are you kidding? Remember fifteen years ago we used to laugh at people eating the placenta after hippie communal births? What's gotten into you?"

Beth holds up the yogurt container. All I can think of

is the Pepsi can that did my stepmother in. I imagine the interior of the yogurt carton, dim light straining in through the waxy white walls, streaks of tissue and blood. Then I picture the inside of the aluminum can: pitch black, metallic, buzzing.

Beth hands me the container. I don't want to take it, but I can't say no. It feels very light, it feels empty. I shake it, tentatively, tilt it back and forth. Then very slowly I open it. I look at Beth and she smiles at me, a smile I cannot read.

There is nothing inside.

THE
SHINING
PATH

AFTER THE FUNERAL, Linda and Toby went straight from the cemetery to La Guardia. Toby said, "One reason to take the boat to Mexico is to not have to go through Queens." Linda didn't know how to reply; after all, she had grown up in Queens and just buried her brother there.

The cabdriver's name was Hamid Ali, and he took some very weird side streets. Changing lanes, he twisted around, and his sullen glittery eyes raked the back seat like bullets. It took all Linda's self-control not to say something to Toby that would somehow let the driver know her brother had just died; perhaps then he would hate them less. Then maybe she could ask him where Muslims believe the spirit goes immediately after death. She wasn't religious or superstitious, but right now she wanted to know. She dreaded the thought of Greg's spirit lurking nearby, shrieking with laughter because on the day of his actual funeral she was taking off for the Yucatán with Toby, who, Greg had always said, had guacamole for brains. If she asked Toby, he would just tell her what the Inca priests believed, and Toby wasn't Inca, so how could he really know? Moving nearer Toby she said, "Are you sure this is okay?"

"There is no okay or not okay," he said. "All you have to do is get through it."

According to Toby, what Linda really needed was a week on top of Machu Picchu. But when they'd totaled their savings, there wasn't nearly enough. Besides, he'd explained, Peru was dangerous now. A guerrilla group called the Shining Path was stopping tourist trains. Linda visualized this so clearly—the screeching brakes, the masked guerrillas emerging from the darkness, the chill of a gun muzzle on her scalp—that she felt certain it would happen, and was relieved when a New Age travel-agent friend of Toby's arranged an amazingly cheap six nights and seven days on an isle off the Yucatán coast.

Though Toby had never been to this island, he'd been almost everywhere else. Toby managed Record Bazaar; it was he who had hired Linda. He knew about all kinds of music—once, when Linda was mad at him, he filled the store with a full day of country-Western begging-and-pleading songs. But the international section was where he could usually be found, picking out CDs to play on the PA. Toby had such great taste that heavy-metal kids were often surprised to find themselves buying the expensive Moroccan joujouka imports he stacked by the cash registers.

On Linda's first day at work, Toby led her through the imports section, past the Greek singers with the Buddy Holly glasses, the colored photos of belly dancers, past the polka bands and the paintings of balalaika players, and put on a CD called *Music from the Andes*. The flute sounded like someone breathing raggedly in your ear. Toby leaned very close and told her that once, in the Andes, he lay awake in his sleeping bag picking out bats with his flashlight, and the next day he overheard some Shirley MacLaine types saying they'd seen the sacred fire birds of the Incas. Later, after they began living together,

Linda heard Toby tell this to other people. He had been to Machu Picchu three times.

At the airport Toby grabbed Linda and rushed to the head of the line. The attendant—who could see that their plane wasn't leaving for hours—glared at them, but checked them in anyhow. Linda knew this was wrong, yet laughed and felt proud of Toby, prouder still when he looked so relaxed while the security guards X-rayed their baggage. Linda fully expected the screen to show the guns and grenades that of course they didn't have.

The last time Linda flew—to her grandmother's funeral in Miami—she was too young to be nervous. But now fear came easily as they boarded the plane. She felt that if she smiled and was appreciative, the plane wouldn't crash, so she thanked the man who checked her boarding pass so profusely that he gave her a funny look. "He thinks you're a hijacker," Toby said.

When the liquor cart came around, Toby bought them each two tequilas. He seemed put out at the cost of the drinks, and complained so loudly that Linda hoped no one heard. In the row behind them, three college girls were painting their fingernails on the tray tables. They giggled and fluttered their coral-tipped fingers as if Linda were a restless child peeking at them through the seats.

La Hacienda del Sol was a clump of thatched adobe huts and one larger hut separated from the beach by a wide patch of oily scrub vegetation. Toby said, "Is this a joke? I thought I was through with this. I thought I'd stayed at my last hippie hammock joint. I'm going to kill Zack. When we get back to the city I'm putting out a contract on him."

A slight, morose-looking man came out of the central building and tipped his straw cowboy hat with an ironic smile—a gesture spoiled somewhat by the way his hat had bunched up his hair so it wound around his head like a turban.

"I am Señor Ramón," he said. "Your host. From where are you coming?"

"Nueva York," said Toby.

"Ah, yes," said Señor Ramón. "New York. I took fifteen credits toward my master's at Columbia."

"What in?" asked Toby, but Señor Ramón had picked up their luggage and set off toward a tiny hut. Inside, the walls were painted a milky poster-paint blue.

"Very cheery," Toby said, but after Señor Ramón left, Toby said, "Hacienda del *Soil*." When Linda didn't answer, Toby said, "Well, I've stayed in worse." After a moment he added: "The Señor looks like he could be pretty bizarre." Bizarre, from Toby, was a term of great approval. It was how he described almost every place he had been.

The bathroom floor was cement, with water pooled in the low spots. Linda got out her flip-flops and went in to take a shower, but Toby stopped her. "Why shower with the ocean outside?" he said. Linda put on her two-piece suit, Toby a pair of trunks in which he looked more

vulnerable than he did naked. Linda, too, felt exposed
—they'd never seen each other in swimsuits. They put
on T-shirts and jeans. "Take your purse," Toby said, and
handed her his traveler's checks, passport, and a frayed
hotel towel.

In front of the largest hut was a thatched ramada and
a Coke machine. Half hidden in the dappled light, Señor
Ramón sat reading. He looked up and waved them over,
asked if they were going swimming and told them about
a quiet cove down the beach.

"What's the shark situation?" Toby said, laughing.

Señor Ramón laughed, too. "They visit from time to
time," he said. "No problem."

Toby set off with Linda trailing several steps behind.
It was a pace they often fell into in the city. There was
a privacy in it Linda liked. They passed some tall empty-
looking hotels, then a fishing village. Some women called
out to them in Spanish. Toby smiled and waved, but the
wind from the ocean was blowing, and Linda forgot to
ask if he understood what they'd said. Linda found a
beautiful shell—pearly, striped yellow and pink. She
picked it up and held it, but when she saw identical shells
everywhere, it no longer seemed worth keeping.

The water was a transparent pale green, slightly rippled
by waves. Linda stared at it a long time, then waded in
up to her ankles. "It's cold," she said, though it wasn't.
"Let me think about this for a while."

Toby swam way out, though never out of sight. Linda
lay down, but each time she closed her eyes, she pictured

watery, blossoming flowers of blood, like in *Jaws*. When she saw Toby heading back, she took off her jeans and shirt and, as he emerged from the water, ran and hugged him. The drops of cold salt water felt wonderful on her skin.

The next day was cloudy and cool. Linda and Toby walked into town. The town was one narrow street which got more crowded with shops selling straw bags and Kahlúa as it neared the zócalo. They passed several restaurants at which Linda would have liked to stop, but Toby crossed the zócalo and kept walking till the street got less fancy again. He led her into a place with no front wall and a damp, outhouse smell. The girl who waited on them was so young the child on her hip could only have been her brother. Toby ordered two coffees and many things they didn't have until the girl nodded yes.

"*Huevos rancheros*," Toby told Linda. "These places are where you get the really fresh tortillas."

After breakfast, they headed toward the far end of the island, where a French couple they'd met the night before had said they could find Mayan ruins. The French tourists were skinny and pale—not entirely well-looking. It turned out they had been traveling for eight years and had been to many of the same places as Toby. During an animated conversation about hepatitis, Linda had gone off to bed.

Linda and Toby overshot the ruins by half a mile till they realized that the pile of stones they'd passed could once have been a lighthouse to guide the Mayan ships.

"We should have gone to Chichén Itzá," Toby said. "Maybe we still should. A real ruin would do you good. The thing about ruins is, you stand there thinking those people were actually here, you feel it, and then you think how all those civilizations have come and gone, so many people have died, that's just the way it is, and it isn't only you. I mean, isn't only *Greg*. Should we go on to Chichén Itzá?"

Linda hadn't been thinking of Greg right then—ever since they'd left New York she'd been trying very hard not to—and now she was a bit startled. She said, "This is fine. Really, Toby. This is perfect." Toby looked at her scornfully. There had been many times when Greg looked at her like that. Remembering this surprised her. She'd imagined that after someone died you'd forget the nastiness and just recall the love, but with Greg she remembered the nastiness, too.

A grassy path led away from the water and along a lagoon. After a long time they stopped for a Sprite and tortillas. Toby showed Linda how to eat tortillas rolled up with white sugar, and a man told them about a bus that would take them near Señor Ramón's.

As soon as they got back, Toby lay down and took a nap. Linda read the guidebook, three pages on the island—mostly descriptions of hotels and restaurants where she now knew she would never eat. She thought, disloyally, that for someone who spent his life in the imports section, Toby showed no interest in tracking down the local mariachis. Perhaps he was worried that music might cost money. She'd never really seen it before, this streak of stinginess in Toby. He'd told her how, in the old days, you could keep traveling as long as you could make your money last. But this clearly wasn't the case—no matter how much money was left, they had to be back Monday. That this should seem comforting made Linda unhappy, and she lay there watching a lizard appear and vanish through a hairline crack in the wall.

Around five, they got up and dressed with vague plans of wandering into town. But as soon as they stepped outside, Señor Ramón came over and asked if they cared for a drink. It was clearly a social invitation, but Linda worried that Toby might misunderstand and ask the Señor how much.

Toby said, "Thank you, we would."

Señor Ramón came back with a tray, three glasses, ice, a bottle of tequila and a bottle of Coke. He mixed drinks—tequila and Coke on ice—and gave them to Linda and Toby. "Mexico Libres," he said. "My invention."

The drink was strong and sweet, and as Linda finished the first and took another, she felt very focused and at the same time very blurred. For once it didn't worry her that she wasn't contributing to the conversation; she liked the low rumbling voices of Toby and Señor Ramón. Toby was saying that they had found the ruins on the beach.

"Oh, *las ruinas*." Señor Ramón laughed. He said these

ruins were nothing; he used to work as a tour guide at Chichén Itzá.

"What a great job that must have been," Toby said. "I've been to Chichén Itzá."

Señor Ramón said, "Great? I have a doctorate in Mayan languages and archaeology, and I worked as a tour guide and now I am managing a hotel. This is a shitty country."

Linda and Toby nodded vigorously. How odd, Linda thought, to be so quick to condemn a place they were paying money to vacation in. Toby said, "What about the U.S.? With a degree like that, you could teach . . ."

"The U.S.," said Señor Ramón, "is a shitty country, too."

"It's a shitty world," Toby said, and the three of them clinked glasses.

All evening, the talk kept circling back to Chichén Itzá, and maybe it was the tequila, but several times, as Señor Ramón described the ruins, Linda wanted to go there, to just get on a bus and go. When she awoke the next morning, she was still thinking of it. But before she could speak, Toby put his arm around her and, settling her head on his chest, said, "Honey, I am hung over. This man needs a day at the beach."

Linda recalled how, when they'd planned this trip, it was all about what *she* needed, the next-best thing after Machu Picchu to help her get over Greg. She, too, felt a little queasy; last night seemed hard to recall. One thing was clear: Señor Ramón had told them it was simple to get to Chichén Itzá—a pleasant ferry trip and an easy bus connection in Valladolid.

"I don't know," Toby said. "I mean, there are ruins and there are ruins. You can spend the day tripping around Chichén Itzá, taking in the beautiful pyramids and the ball court. And then you get to the cenote they threw all the Mayan virgins down, and you look down into the deep black sacrificial well, and it hits you that the entire place was basically about that. It is not for nothing that this whole culture is about panthers and human skulls. Sweetheart, that is *not* what you need."

Linda couldn't quite put this together with what Toby was saying last night to Señor Ramón, or with what he always said about ruins, that the point of them wasn't that something good had happened there, but that people had lived and died there.

"What about Machu Picchu?" she said. "No one got sacrificed there?"

"Those are two totally different stories," Toby said. "For one thing, getting thrown into a well is totally different from getting pitched off the side of a mountain."

In the market, they bought sweet rolls, mangoes, tiny bananas, a hunk of white cheese, and a string bag to carry the food in. Near the ferry dock, Toby rented goggles and a snorkel. He asked Linda if they should rent some for her. She said if she wanted them she would go back. Then they set off for the beach.

As Toby stripped down to his swimsuit, Linda said she

wanted to get really baked before she went into the water. Toby swam off, and she lay down. For some time, her mind drifted pleasantly. But gradually, as the sun heated up, Linda began to sweat. She walked to the water's edge, waded in to her knees, and ran back to dry land.

It began to get very hot. Linda sat up and looked for shade. There had been a time—summers at Yankee Lake, and later, after her father died, Jones Beach with her mother and Greg—when she was always brown. But she had been pale for years, and now she was going to fry. The sensible thing would be to go back to the Hacienda. Would Toby know where to find her? Would he know that she hadn't drowned?

She rolled over onto her stomach and let the sun beat down on her till the inside of her skull felt strongly radioactive. Her mind drifted, first to one thing, then another, then to a particular night—this was when Greg had just gotten sick and moved back in with their mother. His friends visited constantly, so whenever Linda went to her mother's house, it was like time travel back to high school: once more the kitchen table completely surrounded by guys. That night, Greg kept trying to talk about life after death. Their mother kept changing the subject. Greg's friends kept changing it back.

Everyone seemed to have read the same descriptions of the afterlife, reports from people who'd been to the other side and returned to tell the tale. Casually, as if it were a neutral subject, and yet with a special fervor, because it was Greg who had brought it up, who let them offer—no, promise—him comfort, Greg's friends spoke of tunnels leading toward light, paths lined on both sides with radiance. Inside the tunnels echoed God's voice, and all along the light-filled path, your dead, your lost, beloved family and friends welcomed you, smiling.

Greg said he refused to think of the afterlife as *This Is Your Life* with a fog machine and klieg lights. He said he preferred to think of it as eternal Fire Island.

By late afternoon Linda looked boiled. Toby said, "Five seconds more on that beach we'd be talking emergency room." Linda took a cold shower and two aspirins and the swig of paregoric Toby suggested. She was able to dress and go out to eat, though not to taste her food or listen as Toby told her what he'd seen skin diving. All that got through was his description of an octopus hiding its face behind a shell held in its tentacles.

It was Toby's idea to bring home a Coke: if Linda needed more aspirin during the night she'd have something to take it with. Around four, she got up and took two aspirin and then stayed awake drinking Coke. She slept some, and was glad to find it was morning—though she realized that the aspirin must have worn off. Her skin was completely on fire. She took another couple of aspirins but they didn't seem to work. Waiting for Toby to wake just made her sunburn hurt worse. She put on her loosest shirt and shorts and went out into the yard.

The light was already glaring, and the sky looked bleached; she must have slept later than she thought. She was surprised to see Señor Ramón at his table beneath the ramada. He looked up from his book and smiled and toasted her with his coffee cup. There was no way not to go over. She refused coffee, but when he said, "Coca-Cola?" she nodded and sat down.

"What are you reading?" she said.

"Rilke," said Señor Ramón. "*En español*. It is my life ambition to translate Rilke into Mayan." Then he peered at Linda. "You are this sunburned all over?" When she nodded, he made a clicking sound against his teeth.

"I am sorry," he said, in such a stricken tone that Linda said, "Well, it isn't *your* fault."

"Oh, but it is," said Señor Ramón. "I should have realized. It happens all the time. You cannot imagine how often Americans come down on vacation, they have been cold for so long, they get into the sun . . . then . . . just like you. You would think I would know to warn these girls, but that is the selfishness of the human mind, we cannot imagine that someone is truly different from us. Because here, of course, we're dark. Sunburn is not our problem."

"You can't think of everything," Linda said. "You've got enough on your mind."

"Ah," said Señor Ramón. "But this is my country and my hotel. I am a serious host. That is how I am. I cannot stand to see suffering. It is why life is so hard for me. Mostly I am troubled by the sufferings of our poor, and of our educated unemployed young people, but at Chichén Itzá I was unhappy even when one of my elderly tourists would be overcome by heat and have to wait on the bus and miss the pyramids—"

"That's really nice of you," Linda said.

"Nice," said Señor Ramón. There was such a long silence that Linda became uneasy. Finally Señor Ramón smiled a sad, distracted smile and said, "The Mayans had doctors greater than your Houston surgeons. They had uses for more than ten thousand jungle plants. Perhaps in the market . . . or maybe I have some here . . ."

"Excuse me?" said Linda, but Señor Ramón didn't answer. He went into the house and, after a minute, returned with an unlabeled blue bottle.

"For sunburn," he said. "The reason I have it is, so many of my guests, so many Americans, come here and just like you . . ."

"God," Linda said. "Thanks. I can't believe how sweet that is."

"Did you meet Vivian?" he said, and when Linda looked blank, he said, "Of course. Vivian left just before you arrived. Vivian was Canadian, very fair, she got sunburned, worse than you, and I gave her some of this and the next day she was back at the beach . . ." Señor Ramón reached for Linda's hand. "Come," he said, "I will put it on for you."

It hadn't occurred to Linda that Señor Ramón meant anything but to give her the bottle. She said, "Please. Don't bother." Her voice sounded thin, incapable of the mildest resistance as Señor Ramón took her arm.

The last thing Linda wanted was for Señor Ramón to

rub Mayan suntan cure on her. And yet he seemed so sure, as if this were the most ordinary occurrence, a professional matter, something a hotel manager did every day. He made refusing seem childish and absurd, like refusing to open your mouth in the dentist's chair. He made refusing seem unspeakably rude, a paranoid, racist, mean-spirited act that would wound him, make him think she was hesitating because she was American and he was Mexican, because she didn't trust him. Refusing would mark her as the suspicious one, the dirty-minded one, the coward.

The path of least resistance was to let him guide her inside. Linda went slightly numb, like she did before medical checkups, and she told herself that there were health spas all over the world where women paid thousands for skin treatments by much stranger people than Señor Ramón.

The inside of Señor Ramón's house was so dim it took her some time to make out two rooms: a main room with a chair, a table, a hot plate, and farther on, a room with a bed. Señor Ramón sat down on the chair. "Take your clothes off," he said.

"It's okay, I don't need to," said Linda. "My arms and legs are the worst part. The rest really isn't that bad."

"You were wearing a bathing suit?" said Señor Ramón. "No? Please, don't be embarrassed. I am not looking. Don't be silly. Otherwise, we will get medicine on your clothes."

Once more Linda hesitated, and once more the tone

of Señor Ramón's voice made it perfectly clear that this was all business, all health, that there was nothing sexual about it. Anything like that would be strictly in Linda's mind.

Linda took off her clothes and stood naked in front of Señor Ramón. Señor Ramón tipped the bottle and filled his palm with thick pink liquid that looked suspiciously like Pepto-Bismol. He rubbed it into her arms and then into her legs.

Linda held her breath, waiting to see how he touched her. But there was nothing sexual, nothing even remotely suggestive in his soothing but slightly impersonal touch. There was one moment, one moment, as he worked his way toward the sharp demarcations left by her bathing suit—he hesitated, then stopped. It was a mere split second, but it scared her, it gave her the chills. Then Señor Ramón lifted his hand and, with swift light strokes of his fingers, rubbed gingerly and even a little angrily away from her bathing-suit lines.

Linda stood very still and thought of a morning she'd walked into Greg's hospital room and found her mother rubbing lotion on him, for his lesions. Linda had stopped in the doorway, hearing a voice in her brain chant: Forget this, forget. But of course she hadn't forgotten, and she realized now that she wouldn't forget, that this memory had trailed her to Mexico, to this dim room where she stood naked before a stranger who would never know Greg, or what any of them had been through.

Señor Ramón said, "You have had a death in your family."

Linda didn't ask how he knew. He would say Toby told him. He would say he could tell from her skin tone. What difference did it make? It occurred to her that this was the sleaziest thing she had ever heard, asking about Greg's death while rubbing Pepto-Bismol into her naked flesh. And yet she was so relieved that he knew, and that she no longer had to pretend to be a normal person on vacation. It felt luxurious and almost sinful to throw herself on Señor Ramón's sympathy, on their common humanity, on the losses that happen to all of us, regardless of country or race.

"Yes," she said. "My brother."

Señor Ramón said, "You Americans. You know, many times when I studied in your country, people—and I am talking here about graduate students, professors, the so-called intelligentsia—these people would ask me, 'Tell us the truth now. Why is your Mexican culture so morbid? So obsessed with death? All those skulls and snakes and skeletons and . . .' And I would think, You lucky people—you live in a country where no one ever dies."

Linda just looked at him. And after a while Señor Ramón said, "I am very sorry. I must remember that you are not Uncle Sam." Then he suggested that she put her clothes back on. He told her that her sunburn would feel better in a few hours and asked if she didn't feel better already.

"Yes," Linda said, "I do." And in fact it was blissfully painless to put on her clothes and walk out.

But when she got back to her room, she felt worse. The sight of Toby sleeping, curled up, the grayish sheets, clothes strewn everywhere—everything shamed her now, and she understood that she had been a fool, standing there naked, letting a stranger touch anywhere he pleased. She felt a flush, then a tingling all over, a prickling that so terrified her that it was a great relief to remember that she was sunburned. After a while the tingling turned to pain, and she sat down and waited for Toby.

She imagined telling Toby what had happened. Toby would laugh, especially when he figured out that nothing really serious had occurred. He would tease her and make Pepto-Bismol jokes, and now whenever they saw Señor Ramón, they would make Pepto-Bismol jokes behind his back. Laughter would make her feel better, would prove to her that none of this was important.

She was glad she had Toby and could tell him this, that he wouldn't get angry or jealous, like another guy might. She could tell Toby anything. Or almost anything. She wouldn't know how to explain that she'd told Señor Ramón about Greg. Nor could she tell Toby of how she had been reminded of her mother in Greg's hospital room. She hadn't told Toby about that at the time. He didn't want to hear. He had made it very clear to her that he didn't want to hear. There is no one I can tell this to, Linda thought, and for a moment she felt quite breathless.

Linda got up and went out. She walked toward the beach. She stared straight ahead and turned up the shore toward the ruins. Someone shouted to her, but she didn't hear, she looked neither right nor left; the only sound was the ocean.

She kept walking. She grew tired and knew she should turn around. Perhaps she passed the ruins, perhaps not. She felt herself slip comfortably into a staggery zombie gait. The sun was very hot, and there was no breeze from the sea.

Linda kept walking. The light grew brighter until it seemed to her that there was nothing before her but a strip of light with dark bands on both sides. At first she knew that these bands of light and dark were the beach and the sky and the sea, but after some time she forgot that, and it was just a strip of light. Everything shimmered with heat, but still she kept walking, imagining now that faces appeared along both sides of the light, not waving or greeting her but just looking, silently moving their lips but not speaking, like people you see when you're swimming, talking mutely on shore.

Wasn't this what she'd heard about death—that long road of light lined with faces? Was it possible that she was dying? There was so much here that could kill you —sunstroke, scorpions, sharks, disease, poison suntan lotion. She thought: How funny that Greg should be right—death *was* like Fire Island. But if this was death, why weren't the faces welcoming—why didn't they know who she was?

Linda looked for Greg, but he wasn't there, wasn't

anywhere. If this was the afterlife, what had happened to her brother? And it was his absence that finally convinced her: this bright, endless road of light and indifferent faces wasn't death after all, but a vision of life, of this moment—a picture, clear as a photograph, of what lay around and before her, of how little would be familiar to her and of all she had yet to go through.

HANSEL

AND

GRETEL

TACKED TO THE WALL of the barn that served as Lucia de Medici's studio were 144 photographs of the artist having sex with her cat. Some of the pictures showed the couple sweetly nuzzling and snuggling; in some Lucia and her black cat, Hecuba, appeared to be kissing passionately, while still others tracked Hecuba's leathery rosebud of a mouth down Lucia's neck to her breasts until the cat disappeared off the edge of the frame and Lucia's handsome head tilted back . . .

This was twenty years ago, but I can still recall the weariness that came over me as I looked at Lucia's photos. I didn't want to have to look at them, particularly not with Lucia watching. I was twenty-one years old. I had been married for exactly ten days to a man named Nelson. It had seemed like a good idea to drop out of college and marry Nelson, and a good idea (it was Nelson's idea) to spend the weekend in Vermont at his friend Lucia's farm. At that time, I often did things because they seemed like a good idea, and I often did very important things for lack of a reason not to.

Lucia de Medici was an Italian countess, a direct descendant of the Florentine ruling family, and a famous conceptual artist. She was also, I'd just discovered, the mother of a woman named Marianna, the love of Nelson's life, an old girlfriend who, until that afternoon, I'd somehow assumed was dead.

Striped by the sunlight filtering in through the gaps between the barn boards, Lucia and I regarded each other: two zebras from different planets. She was a small woman

of about fifty, witchy and despotic, her whole being in-
geniously wired to telegraph beauty and discontent. And
what was Lucia seeing, if she saw me at all? A girl with
the power that came unearned from simply being young
and with every reason not to act like such a quivering
blob of Jell-O.

She said, "Up here in the wilderness I am working so
in isolation, some days I want to ask the cows what do
they think of my art."

"It's . . . really something," I said.

"Meaning what?" Lucia said. I was pleased she cared
what I thought, but hadn't she just explained: when it
came to Lucia's art, the cows' opinion counted? She
frowned. "*Prego*. Watch out, please, not to back up into
the fish tank."

I turned, glad for fish to focus on after Lucia and her
cat. An enormous goldfish patrolled the tank with effi-
cient shark-like menace, while several guppies hovered
in place, rocking oddly from side to side. "I am scared
of that big fish," Lucia confided. "He push his sister out
of the water, I find her gasping dead on the floor."

"Are you sure it wasn't the cat?" I asked.

"Of that I am sure," she said.

I sensed that Lucia had tired of me, and I thought that
now we would leave her studio. Instead, she switched on
the stereo and voices filled the barn. Suddenly my eyes
watered; it was my favorite piece of music, the trio from
Così fan tutte that the women sing when their lovers
are leaving and they beg the wind and water to be good

to them on their way. Their sadness is a painful joke because their lovers aren't leaving but disguising themselves as Albanians and seducing the women as a test, a test the women eventually fail, a painful joke on them all.

I listened to the delicate, mournful tones, the liquid rippling of the strings, cradling and oceanic. There was grief in the women's voices, pitiful because it is wasted, pitiful and humiliating because we know it and they don't.

"It's beautiful," I said.

"So you say now," Lucia said. "This, too, is one of my projects. I think everything gets boring sooner or later, no? The most fantastic Mozart becomes unbearable after a while. So I have put this trio on a loop that plays over and over until the audience cannot stand it and runs screaming out of the room."

Lucia's project depressed me. I felt personally implicated, though I knew: there was no way that she could have had me and Nelson in mind. In the ten days since we'd been married, Nelson had changed so profoundly that he might as well have gone off and come back disguised as an Albanian. You hear women say: Before the marriage my husband never drank or hit me or looked at another woman. But with Nelson there was nothing so violent or dramatic. Before the wedding he'd liked me; afterwards he didn't.

He had been my lab instructor in a college biology course. He was a graduate student in anthropological botany, writing his thesis on the medicinal plants commonly used by the rain-forest tribes he'd lived among for two years. It was rumored that most of his research was on Amazonian hallucinogens, so it made sense that he was often strange, mumbly and withdrawn—but a perfectly capable and popular lab instructor. He was blond and handsome and tall; he looked lovely in a lab coat. He came from an old Boston family and played jazz clarinet.

Right from the start, our love had been tainted with cruelty. My lab partner was a squeamish boy, a Mormon from Idaho, who refused to cut into, or even touch, anything slimy. I enjoyed humiliating him, I feel I have to confess this, so as not to make myself sound nicer or more innocent than I was. From the other side of the lab table Nelson watched me grab the etherized frog from my partner's shaky hands, and our eyes locked in the candle-like glow of the Bunsen burners. Later, Nelson told me that what had caught his attention was that my lab partner was in love with me and I had no idea. I believed that Nelson imagined this, but even so I was flattered—flattered and guilty and proud, all at once, for having made the Mormon boy suffer.

Nelson was moody, given to brooding silences in which I knew he was grieving over Marianna. He didn't like to talk about her or about his time in the jungle. I'd never met a man with a past he didn't like to discuss, or for that matter a man with any past at all. Nothing had ever happened to the boys I knew in college, but they were so touchingly eager to tell you all about it. I was young enough to be enthralled by what a man wouldn't say, and I believed the glitter dust of romance and adventure would sprinkle on me like confetti if I stood close enough to Nelson.

Marianna had gone with Nelson to the Amazon, but she was demonically restless, she'd left and flown back every few months. Nelson said he always *knew* the night before she arrived. She used to hitchhike in with bush pilots who invited her along because she was so beautiful—beautiful and doomed.

"If those pilots knew her," Nelson said, "they wouldn't have taken her up in an elevator. Every time a plane took off, she was praying it would crash. She had a death wish instead of a conscience, she was born suicidal, it was a miracle she lasted long enough to meet me. Her suicide attempts got more and more serious until I couldn't do anything to . . ." His voice trailed off and he took a deep breath that ended the conversation.

I don't know why I assumed from this that Marianna was dead. It helped, I suppose, that I was never able to ask the obvious questions: when and where Marianna died, and how exactly she did it. Instead, I went through Nelson's possessions. I found his journal from the Amazon, and nowhere—nowhere—in it was one word about Marianna. Stupidly, this cheered me; it made her seem less important. I thought I'd learned something new about her, not something new about Nelson.

He told me I made him happy. He said we should get married. He said we shouldn't tell anyone, not even our parents or friends. I agreed, though it bothered me, not being able to boast that I'd been chosen by a handsome older man, the most popular lab instructor. In City Hall, we ducked behind a door when Nelson saw a judge who knew his father; and that was the last time he touched me, yanking me out of the judge's way.

For a week after the wedding he paced our hot cramped Cambridge apartment, staying up all night, listening to music: Bill Evans, Otis Redding, Bach—only the slow second movements. I couldn't ask him what was wrong, if he thought we'd made a mistake. It didn't take a genius to draw the logical conclusion when someone seemed so much happier before getting married—to you. I was not supposed to notice that I was sleeping alone in the bed that had also changed unrecognizably, grown colder and less welcoming since when we used to spend all day there.

One morning Nelson brought me coffee. He said he knew he'd been rotten and he was mightily sorry. He said he'd eaten some things in the jungle that he shouldn't have eaten, and now he had these episodes, he was gone for days at a time.

"Episodes?" I said. "Gone?" Why hadn't he ever had one in all the months we'd lived together?

Nelson said we needed to get away: an impromptu honeymoon in Vermont. That morning we threw our knapsacks into his VW Bug. We drove with the windows open, my long hair streaming back, and for a time I felt we'd left our problems behind in Cambridge, along with my toothbrush and contact-lens fluid and everything else

I needed. I kept wondering about Nelson's episodes. Did he have them when he was driving?

Early in the afternoon we turned into Lucia's long, tree-lined driveway, which, Nelson said, always reminded him of the stately avenues of lime trees leading to Tolstoy's estate.

"How do you know Lucia?" I asked.

"Mutual friends," he said.

Lucia ran out of the rambling spotless white farmhouse and kissed Nelson three times, alternating cheeks, then grabbed his shoulders and gave him a smacky kiss on the mouth. She eyed me coolly, then smiled flirtatiously at Nelson, as if he'd come to amuse her by showing off his very large new pet.

"What's this?" she said.

"Polly. My new wife," he said. "Polly, this is Lucia."

"Your new *what*?" Lucia asked, only slightly dimming my pleasure in his finally having told someone. "Welcome." She embraced me swiftly, kissing my sweaty forehead.

"Guess what?" she asked Nelson. "Just yesterday I got a postcard from Marianna. She is in India at an ashram, fucking hundreds of people a day. She writes she is finding enlightenment through nonstop tantric fucking."

Nelson touched the top of his car. His hand came away black with grime, and for a moment the three of us stood there staring at his hand. "I'm sorry," Lucia said. "But if I can't tell you, who can I tell? All alone I am going crazy."

"Marianna?" I said.

"My daughter," said Lucia. "Nelson's friend."

I couldn't stop myself from saying, "But I thought she was dead!"

"My daughter is very much alive, thank you. Nelson, what have you been telling this child? Anyway, it is perfect you come. Marianna sends me a phone number where I can call her in India this weekend, we can go into town where is the nearest phone."

"There's no phone here?" I said.

"Of course not," said Lucia. "Now come to my studio and see my new piece. I call it *Così fan tutte*, starring me and my cat."

Nelson said he'd see it later, he needed to walk, he'd been in the car all morning; Lucia tried not to look disappointed at being left with me. Nelson headed off toward a horse barn and Lucia led me across a field on a path tunneled between high grasses. I didn't know what to say. I felt I should praise everything I could—nice house, nice land, nice view, nice sky—without sounding truly psychotic. Finally I said, "What beautiful blue flowers!" The field was completely blue.

"Bachelor's buttons." Lucia sighed. "In Europe they are weeds. For years I never grow them. Then I learn they keep their color forever, Etruscan tombs are full of them, Etruscans bury them with their dead to stay blue in the afterlife."

For an instant the waves of heat shimmering over the field resolved into a miniature phantom funeral procession, Etruscans in white, bearing scythes and armloads of blue flowers; and in that instant I wondered if Nelson's episodes might be catching.

Then we went to Lucia's studio and looked at the photos of her and her cat, and she played the Mozart that we listened to over and over. I could have listened forever and never gotten tired and been grateful for every minute by which it shortened the weekend. But after four or five times I said, "Okay! Enough!" It seemed required, like my admiring the field of blue flowers.

Lucia switched off the stereo and said, "I am right, am I not? Now go find Nelson, and I will do another five minutes more work."

But it was five hours before Lucia emerged from her studio and found us on the lawn, bouncing grumpily in our metal armchairs. We had been arguing about Lucia, furiously but without speaking, so perhaps only I was arguing and Nelson was thinking about something else.

Finally—after a walk through the scratchy fields matted with treacherous berry canes, and a long nap that Nelson took and I wasn't invited to join—I'd mentioned the photos of Lucia and her cat. I suppose I expected some conspiratorial expression of normal distaste.

Instead, Nelson said, "I love her. She's absolutely bananas." I recalled the lab partner I'd nearly dissected for Nelson's benefit, and now I needed Nelson, and he was taking Lucia's side. But there was no comparison. Lucia wasn't some squeamish kid who made you do all his experiments for him. Lucia was Nelson's very good friend and former mother-in-law.

I had spent Nelson's nap time in the airless library with its motley collection of books, tattered and reeking of mildew. These were mostly in Italian but there were also some volumes in English on folklore, magic, and witch-craft. It was no accident that I was drawn to a volume of *Grimm's Fairy Tales*, nor was it accidental that I turned to "Hansel and Gretel" and read it for survival tips as much as for entertainment. This was the version in which the witch is fattening up the children and feeling the chicken bones Gretel holds out to deceive the witch into thinking the children are still thin.

After I mentioned the cat photos and Nelson defended Lucia, I thought how different the story would be if Hansel were in collusion with the witch. So when at last Lucia appeared from her studio and said, "You children must be starving! I will make chicken with mushrooms," I must have paled. Lucia said, "Nelson, look, your friend is half dead already from hunger."

"No," I said, "I'm not, I'm fine, I'm not hungry at all."

Inside the house we found Hecuba licking a stick of butter on the dining-room table. Lucia buried her face in the cat's black fur and, with many tiny kisses, set it on the floor. She opened a bottle of wine and put two glasses on the kitchen table.

"From the state liquor store," she said. "Imagine such a thing! I think it is so that they can keep track of how much and what we are drinking. Now you two sit down. In the kitchen, I am a wild woman. A maniac. Watch out."

With that, she began to fly about, chopping, stirring, frying. "After dinner we will phone Marianna," she said. "When it is seven here, I think, is nine in India."

Lucia reached up and took down one of several large apothecary jars full of what appeared to be dried lizards. "My mushrooms," she said. "My beauties. I could kiss each one. This has been a fabulous year. Tonight with the chicken I will put in maybe eight kinds of mushrooms I find in the woods this spring."

"Do you . . . know a lot about mushrooms?" I couldn't hide the tremor in my voice.

Lucia laughed. "Nelson has eaten my mushrooms for years, and he is alive to tell the tale. Don't worry, every mushroom I pick, I send a spore print to Washington for analysis. No one knows you can do this, but it is the only safe way. I have a good friend, he finds mushrooms all his life, last spring he eats something he has been picking for years, he barely has time to call Poison Control before he loses all sensation in his—"

"I've got an idea," said Nelson. "We feed Polly first and then watch her for twenty-four hours to see if she makes it."

It was the sort of intimate teasing that married couples indulge in, and I might have been encouraged that Nelson was choosing to do it if I hadn't suspected that they were capable of sitting at the table, discussing Nelson's research, Lucia's art, and occasionally checking to see if I had survived the dinner. It crossed my mind that if I did die from mushroom poisoning, I would at least be spared going into town and phoning Marianna.

It was reassuring that we all started eating at once, food that was so delicious, who cared if it was lethal? Behind Nelson was a window and all through dinner I'd been distracted by dark shapes swooping near the glass.

"What kind of birds are those?" I finally asked.

"Bats, darling," said Lucia. "But my bats are very strange bats. Most bats squeak, you know, like mice. But my bats cry like kitties. Isn't that right, Hecuba, my love? Tell our friends what the little bats say."

Lucia couldn't remember if she had gas in her car, so we took Nelson's VW, with our sleeping bags still in back. I offered Lucia the front seat. I was shocked when she accepted. Since then I have met others who take you up on what's only politeness; it's like some spiteful playground trick you fall for again and again. I scrunched up in the back seat: a relief, in a way.

Lucia slid in front and said, "I don't believe in seat belts. To me, is a fascist plot."

Then the whole grim scenario played out before my eyes, Nelson having an episode, Lucia not wearing her seat belt. Was it more or less scary that this was wishful thinking on my part? I felt like a child in the back seat, sullen and resentful. I thought mean thoughts about Lucia and Nelson, that they had more in common than just

Hansel and Gretel

Marianna. By temperament, they were spoilers, they enjoyed ruining your pleasure, making you hate what you might otherwise love: Mozart, bachelor's buttons, mushrooms, food . . . in Nelson's case, my whole life.

For just the briefest moment, I was sorry for Marianna. And suddenly I felt frightened, alone, at Lucia and Nelson's mercy, like a heroine in a thriller, Ingrid Bergman in *Notorious*, held prisoner in South America by Claude Rains and his evil mother. But Lucia and Nelson weren't conspiring to kill me. It was fine with them, enough for them, to make me acutely unhappy. Though it wasn't —ever—clear to me if they even knew, or cared.

It was a soft July evening. We drove along a river, past a waterfall. Light and water splashed on us, beading up on the car. A valley opened before us, rolling fields studded with barns, silos, farmhouses, kitchen gardens: quiet façades behind which families and household pets must have been eating dinner, inside, out of the golden light.

"Look!" I said, unnecessarily. Nelson and Lucia were already staring at a blazing wedge of sun streaming down from one high cloud.

"People say I am imagining," said Lucia. "But I know for a fact I am psychic. Yesterday morning I woke up and I knew I would hear from Marianna though it was, oh Jesus Christ, early spring since I hear from her last. That time she turned on the gas in your apartment, Nelson, I was at a party in Manhattan, and at the very moment my daughter was trying to kill herself, I suddenly faint and throw up all over the dinner table."

223

There was a silence. Nelson said, "Two hundred years ago my ancestors would have burned women like you and Marianna at the stake."

Now I was glad that I was in the back, I could burrow down in the lumpy seat and try not to be hurt that Nelson's forebears wouldn't have wasted their time burning a woman like me.

"So would the people in this town," Lucia said. "They would boil me in oil on Main Street if they knew anything about me."

Only then did I realize that we *were* in town. On the way to Lucia's, Nelson and I had passed many pretty country villages crowded with tourist couples shopping for maple products. But Lucia's town wasn't one of those. Two grim rows of water-stained Greek Revival houses led up to the business section, a dusty crossroads—gas station, post office, grocery, hardware—uninterested in a stranger's patronage or in any hospitable cosseting frills, like, for example, a sidewalk. I tried to imagine a life for myself and Nelson in such a town, in one of the nicer houses, near somewhere he could teach . . . but it didn't seem like a good idea, thinking too far into the future.

"If they knew . . ." Lucia said darkly. "About me and Hecuba . . . and my work. It is very anarchist, very un-Puritan and subversive. But to them I am just a crazy Italian, her house always needs fixing, her checks clear at the bank. Meanwhile, they tell me the gossip, the carpenters and electricians and plumbers. This town is a pit of snakes."

What people was she talking about? There was no one in this town, no children wheeling on their bikes as their parents watered the shaggy lawns. It was as if a bomb had dropped while we were out at Lucia's, and we hadn't known about it, and we were the only ones left.

"Turn here," Lucia instructed Nelson. Nelson pulled up to the grocery, a one-story brick-red cinder-block structure streaked with patches of oily black. Against the wall was a phone booth and a rickety picnic bench with an uninterrupted view of the gas pump.

"Oh God! Oh God! Oh God!" cried Lucia.

"What is it?" Nelson said, and from the back seat I echoed lamely, "What's wrong?"

"I forget my money. We must go home. I will miss Marianna!"

"I have money," said Nelson. "Can you get change in the store?"

"I can try." Lucia rolled her head and flared her nostrils, breathing harshly. I felt as if I were in the car with a small pony starting to panic. "Two women work here, sisters, one nice, one bitch, you never know who you are getting . . ."

Nelson handed her a bill. "It's a ten," he said.

"I know that," snapped Lucia, groping for the door handle.

Nelson leaned across her. Presumably he meant to open the door, but he was restraining her, too. He had to twist around slightly. I was shocked by the look on his face. I was afraid he was having an episode. Then something in his expression reminded me of my lab partner in the split second he had to decide whether to relinquish the frog or fetal pig I was grabbing out of his hands. Briefly I wondered if Nelson had been right about the Mormon boy's secret passion for me. Because suddenly I recognized the expression of a man who has just realized that he will—that he is helpless not to—humiliate himself for love. And that was *my* psychic moment: I knew what was going to happen. I knew what Nelson was going to say long before he was able to make himself sound even slightly casual.

Nelson said, "Say hello to Marianna. Tell her I'm up here visiting with my new wife."

"Yes, of course," Lucia said and jumped out of the car.

The summer evening was warm and pretty, but Nelson and I stayed in the car. I didn't move up front. We stared at the storefront, on which there was nothing to see, not even a beer or cigarette ad or a sign announcing a special. Eventually Lucia appeared, holding a small paper bag. She gave us the V-sign and dipped her hand into the bag. The last rays of dusky evening light shone on the silver quarters raining back into the sack. I thought of how "Hansel and Gretel" ends with a shower of pearls and jewels that the children steal from the witch and play with when they get home.

As if we were at a drive-in movie, we watched Lucia kneel and gather some coins she'd dropped, then stuff them in the phone, and dial and listen and slam the coin return and begin all over again . . .

"You know, it's the strangest thing," I said. "I thought Marianna was dead."

"Dead?" said Nelson. "Right on the edge, and the worst part is, she could live on that edge till she's ninety. What else do you think she's doing, fucking an entire ashram in Bombay? Just *being* in Bombay. She got sick as a dog every time she came down to see me in the jungle. Once she found this empty patch of jungle and was squatting there puking and shitting and she looked up and saw a viper coiled around a branch just over her head."

In theory Nelson was talking to me, but he was looking at Lucia. And now it seemed, unbelievably, Lucia had placed her call. She was talking rapidly, gesticulating . . . She turned her back to us and leaned into the wall and bent her head as she listened and shouted . . .

At last Lucia got back in the car. "Okay, we go home now," she said.

This silence lasted the longest. "What did she say?" Nelson asked.

"Nothing," replied Lucia. "I couldn't reach her. That was someone at the ashram, a man who speaks Italian. Yes, they know her very well there. She has just left for the Himalayas. She will stay in the mountains until fall . . ."

We drove back to Lucia's, and when we got out of the car, Lucia said, "I am tired now. You can sleep in my studio. There is a little mattress with sheets and also towels. The first light switch inside the door."

Nelson bent to kiss Lucia good night. Lucia turned away.

A full moon was shining on the fields. We didn't stop to admire it. I tried a timid werewolf howl, but Nelson didn't laugh. He was walking ahead of me; he knew the way to the barn, which had cooled off considerably since that afternoon.

The switch lit an old-fashioned bedside lamp on a table near a mattress that Lucia had made up with pillows, clean white sheets, and a thin red quilt. She must have done it some time before she left the studio to cook dinner, just when I was assuming she'd forgotten us completely.

The lamp threw out a circle of light, thankfully too modest to include the photos of the artist and her cat, or the killer fish in his tank. I didn't want to see those pictures now, I didn't want to feel jealous because Lucia's passion for her cat was deeper and more tender than what Nelson felt for me.

I shucked off my clothes and slid under the quilt. Nelson waited a moment. Then he took off his jeans and got into bed in his T-shirt and shorts. He rolled over so his back was to me.

"Good night, Polly," he said.

"Good night," I said.

"I love you," he said.

"I love you, too," I said.

I think he may have fallen asleep. I remember that he slept. I turned off the night-light; bars of moonlight took its place. I lay in the dark and listened to the cat, mewing like a newborn, a cry that seemed to get louder when I realized it might be a bat.

Hansel and Gretel

I wished I could have found the switch on Lucia's stereo that activated the endless loop of the Mozart trio. It didn't matter how often I'd heard it, I couldn't remember it now when I most needed its soothing distractions. I wished I could recall exactly how it sounded, the voices of the women with their misdirected grief, each mourning because she imagines her lover is facing the dangers of travel, when her true misfortune is beyond what she can imagine: the cruelty of a lover who would want to test her like that.

Twenty years later I went with my second husband and our children to visit friends in Vermont. Over dinner our friend reminisced about the past, the years when the woods in every direction were teeming with crazy artists. He mentioned people we all knew, who had lived there for a while . . .

My attention had drifted, lulled by the pleasures of friends, food and wine, the distant shouts of children on the lawn, the sweet light of that summer evening. Then once more I had a moment when I knew what was going to happen, that my friend was about to mention an Italian woman artist who had lived just through the forest, essentially next door . . .

I had forgotten, I never exactly knew, where precisely Lucia lived. And I wasn't thinking about that long-ago night at her house until the moment—that is, the instant before—my friend mentioned Lucia de Medici's name.

I said, "I used to know her. I spent a weekend at her

farm." And everybody stared at me, because my voice shook so.

There was a second coincidence, a shadow of the first. For dinner that night we were having chicken with wild mushrooms. For all I knew, our hostess had picked the mushrooms in the woods, but when I asked where the mushrooms came from and she heard my concern, she made a point of saying how much they cost, dried, in the store, because she knew that the fact of a store would reassure someone like me. To my friends, my having spent a weekend with their former neighbor was no more remarkable than having chicken with mushrooms twice in twenty years.

And really, it wasn't surprising for adults to know someone in common; by then the threads of our lives had stretched long enough to have converged at various places. But what shocked me was that my friends had known someone who seemed to belong to a whole other existence. I felt as if I'd been reincarnated and just now recognized the entire cast from my previous life: shuffled, playing brand-new parts, living in different houses.

I said, "Whatever happened to her? To Lucia?"

My friend said, "She went back to Italy. I think I heard something like that."

"Did you ever meet her daughter?" I said.

"Her daughter?" My friend considered. "Oh, yes, she had a crazy daughter. Lucia was always worrying. She was always in some nutty place, Machu Picchu or Kathmandu . . ."

"Was the daughter beautiful?" I said.

"Beautiful?" my friend repeated. "Sort of pretty, I guess. Very nervous, overbred . . . like a big trembly Afghan hound."

Then my friend mentioned another friend, a mutual friend, a friend so close our families often spent holidays together. And it seemed that this friend had also been a neighbor of Lucia's. He had also lived on a farm, but on the other side, and had lived there that same summer, perhaps that very same weekend. Did I know that? our host asked.

But how could I have known that? How could I have understood that two messengers from my future were, even as I lay awake in that barn, just beyond the hedge? I wondered how often the future waits on the other side of the wall, knocking very quietly, too politely for us to hear, and I was filled with longing to reach back into my life and inform that unhappy girl: all around her was physical evidence proving her sorrows would end. I wanted to tell her that she would be saved, but not by an act of will: clever Gretel pretending she couldn't tell if the oven was hot and tricking the witch into showing her and shoving the witch in the oven. What would rescue her was time itself and, above all, its inexorability, the utter impossibility of anything ever staying the same.

But I—that is, the girl I was—couldn't possibly have heard. She was too busy listening for the mewing of cats, or bats. To have even tried to tell her would be like rising up out of the audience just when those angelic voices are praying for gentle winds, a calm ocean, like interrupting the opera to comfort or warn the singers: Don't worry, there is no journey, no one is going away, there is nothing to fear but your own true love, disguised as an Albanian.

BOOKS BY FRANCINE PROSE

A CHANGED MAN
A Novel
ISBN 0-06-019674-2 (New in hardcover)

"Riotously funny . . . Prose uses humor to light up key social issues, to skewer smugness, and to create characters whose flaws only add to their depth and richness." —*Booklist* (starred review)

THE LIVES OF THE MUSES
Nine Women & the Artists They Inspired
ISBN 0-06-055525-4 (paperback)

A brilliant, wry, and deliberately provocative examination of the complex relationship between the artist and his muse.

"A wonderful work of revisionist biography." —*Kirkus Reviews*

BLUE ANGEL
A Novel
ISBN 0-06-095371-3 (paperback)

Deliciously risqué, *Blue Angel* is a withering take on modern academic mores.

National Book Award Finalist in Fiction

GUIDED TOURS OF HELL
Novellas
ISBN 0-06-008085-X (paperback)

"Irresistibly readable. . . . Wit, knowingness, and an intimate familiarity with guilt and anxiety—Francine Prose has these qualities in abundance."
—David Lodge, *New York Times Book Review*

THE PEACEABLE KINGDOM
Stories
ISBN 0-06-075404-4 (paperback)

"Smartly observed and deftly written, these eleven stories present the weird jungle of modern life through the eyes of a wry and mordant writer." —*New York Times Book Review*

WOMEN AND CHILDREN FIRST
Stories
ISBN 0-06-050728-4 (paperback)

"A meticulously observed collection . . . Stories that glow with a burnished wisdom." —*New York Times*

HOUSEHOLD SAINTS
A Novel
ISBN 0-06-050727-6 (paperback)

"Prose brings off a minor miracle of her own in the rare sympathy and detachment with which she gives life to his poignant story. She writes equally well about sausages and saints."
—Jean Strouse, *Newsweek*

PRIMITIVE PEOPLE
A Novel
ISBN 0-06-093469-7 (paperback)

"Francine Prose has a wickedly sharp ear for pretentious American idiom, and no telling detail escapes her observation."
—*New York Times Book Review*

BOOKS FOR YOUNG READERS

THE DEMONS' MISTAKE
A Story From Chelm
ISBN 0-688-17565-1 (Greenwillow hardcover)

The mischievous demons of Chelm, the legendary town in Poland where only fools live, wreak havoc on a daily basis.

YOU NEVER KNOW
A Legend of the Lamed-vavniks
ISBN 0-688-15806-4 (Greenwillow hardcover)

The town of Plotchnik hasn't had a drop of rain in forty days. But the town's humble shoemaker, Poor Schmuel, has the power to command rain and much more.

AFTER
A Novel
ISBN 0-06-008081-7 (Joanna Cotler Books hardcover)

A chilling novel about the aftermath of a high school shooting, and what happens when personal freedoms are extinguished in the name of security.

Don't miss the next book by your favorite author.
Sign up for AuthorTracker by visiting *www.AuthorTracker.com*.

Available wherever books are sold, or call 1-800-331-3761 to order.